11-10

D1483281

THE SUITOR LIST

Other books by Shirley Marks:

An Agreeable Arrangement
Geek to Chic
His Lordship's Chaperone
Honeymoon Husband
Lady Eugenia's Holiday
Miss Quinn's Quandary

THE SUITOR LIST

•

Shirley Marks

AVALON BOOKS
NEW YORK

Published by Avalon Books,
an imprint of Thomas Bouregy & Co., Inc.
160 Madison Avenue, New York, NY 10016

Library of Congress Cataloging-in-Publication Data

Marks, Shirley.
    The suitor list / Shirley Marks.
        p. cm.
    ISBN 978-0-8034-7796-4 (acid-free paper)   1. Aristocracy
(Social class)—England—Fiction.   2. London (England)—
Social life and customs—19th century—Fiction.   3. Courtship—
Fiction.   I. Title.
    PS3613.A7655S85 2010
    813'.6—dc22

                                                                2010018322

PRINTED IN THE UNITED STATES OF AMERICA
ON ACID-FREE PAPER
BY HADDON CRAFTSMEN, BLOOMSBURG, PENNSYLVANIA

To Gusta and her mother, Kim, for their inspiration

*   *   *

A special acknowledgment to my fellow
Avalon author Beate Boeker and her Latin
teacher, Jürgen Wagner, for their assistance

Chapter One

Oh, Moo, do put that book away." Seated at her usual spot at breakfast, Lady Augusta Worth turned a page of the *La Belle Assemblée* magazine before her. "It is exceedingly rude to read at the table."

"And what are you doing, pray? Browsing fashion plates is equally as impolite." Muriel sat directly across from her eldest sister. She placed her morning correspondence in her book, marking her place, flipped it closed with a snap, and glared.

"It is most certainly of no consequence to you, but as I am to come out this year, I must have all new gowns and a court dress for when I am presented to the Queen!"

Fair-haired Charlotte, the middle sister, remained quiet during the heated exchange and demurely gazed into her porridge bowl while nibbling on a corner of dry toast.

"The Queen!" Muriel snorted.

"I'm sure the Queen shan't want a determined bluestocking such as you presented, I daresay." Augusta placed her napkin next to her plate.

1

"I'm twelve!" Muriel cried out.

Charlotte looked up from her bowl and stared across the table, seemingly out the large picture window across from her that faced the expanse of the front drive of Faraday Hall.

She had the peculiar talent of holding her left eye perfectly still while moving her right eye outward with a decided twitch. The effect was quite unsettling at the least and wholly disturbing in the extreme.

Her right eye began to quiver and it alone moved to stare at the eldest sister while her left eye remained quite still and continued to look out the picture window.

"Stop it, Char-Char!" Augusta brought her hands to her eyes, shielding the middle sister from view.

Muriel laughed out loud. "Oh, Char-Char, that is famous!"

Charlotte closed her eyes, pressing her palms to her lids, and chuckled. Performing the quivering eye trick kept her eyes open for such an extraordinary amount of time it made them ache.

"Stop it! Stop it!" Augusta turned to scold her. "No one will want you if they see you do that!"

"And you know all there is about being a *real* lady, don't you, Gusta?" Muriel slipped from her chair and swept her book off the table and into her arms.

"Oh, Moo, you just—"

"Girls!" Their aunt, Mrs. Penelope Parker, stood at the doorway. Her lace cap and somber attire indicated her widow status. In reality, she was not much older than Augusta. "Please, *ladies* do not go on so."

Augusta straightened and sniffed in what she must have considered victory.

Charlotte gave a little sigh, displaying innocence.

Muriel, definitely the more precocious of the three nieces, made a triumphant chuckle and offered a self-satisfied smile.

"Tell them," Augusta demanded in a straightforward manner. "Tell them both!"

Aunt Penny dispensed herself a cup of coffee from the urn on the sideboard while her eldest niece continued.

"*I* am going to Town." Augusta's tirade did not ebb. "*I* am going to be presented. *I* am to find a husband. *I* am to be the first one to be *married*."

"Well, *you* have to be the first because if any man sets eyes upon Char-Char before making your acquaintance, no one will want you!" Muriel added to her sister's diatribe with precision timing, knowing exactly what to say.

"That will be quite enough, Muriel!" Aunt Penny scolded.

"Tell Moo she's not going because she's just a silly little girl. Not to mention *childish*!" Augusta glared at her youngest sister. "Char can't go because—" Well . . . because Muriel had been correct about their middle sister.

On first sight there was no denying that shy, unassuming Charlotte was a diamond of the first water. Everyone who was acquainted with their family knew it to be true. And if Augusta were to make a match, she needed to be without Charlotte, who would surely lure all the men away.

"We are to leave for Town in two months' time," Aunt Penny announced, occupying the chair next to Charlotte.

"Two months?" Augusta stood, clearly outraged. She

would miss the beginning entirely. "The Season begins in just over a fortnight. We should leave in a day or two. What does Papa have to say about this?"

"Your father and I have given your coming out, for each of your entrées into Society, great consideration. We must be very careful . . ." Aunt Penny was their mother's youngest sibling. She had also grown up in a family with three beautiful sisters and knew where the difficulties lay.

"Do you not know what a catch you are? All of you." Aunt Penny stared at each one in turn. "You have connections, beauty, position. Your father, His Grace, and I have done our best to shield you from the influences of the outside world. But now you are young ladies, nearly all at the age to consider marriage. There are men out there, not all of them *gentlemen*."

Augusta, Charlotte, and Muriel exchanged glances.

"Some men would seek you out because you three have beauty beyond compare. To some undesirable suitors your dowry is more than a modest fortune they cannot ignore. And some would wish for the excellent connections that marriage into the Duke's family would bring." Aunt Penny leaned back in her chair and continued. "His Grace, your father, has bestowed upon you everything he has—his love and attention. He has spared no expense in your education."

A groan emanated from Muriel, followed by an animated gaze heavenward.

"All of you are accomplished—oh, dear, yes, I should say so. In dance, music, various artistic achievements, and languages. Your manners, deportment, and character are without equal. Any gentleman would—should feel honored to have you for a wife—you mustn't forget that." Aunt Penny's eyes seemed to mist over. "You deserve the best. Why should you not make a love match? Do you not recall how your own parents had been? They were very happy, indeed."

Before Mama died, Augusta mused. And look at Papa now. Alone, with only his four children to give him joy. Fredrick, his only son, had already flown the nest to attend Eton. What would happen to their father when his daughters had all married and left?

"I know what difficulties lie ahead." Aunt Penny regarded each of her nieces, who stared back in wide-eyed fascination. "You must be cautious in choosing, for once married you are at the mercy of your husband.

"The highest ranking are not always the most worthy and you may not find their ilk agreeable," she cautioned her nieces. "Even you may not know who will win your heart. You must remember that you *always* have a choice. Do not allow anyone to tell you otherwise."

"Good afternoon, Charlotte." Richard Wilbanks escorted his eldest sister, Emily, into the Blue Parlor of Faraday Hall.

"Isn't this all so very exciting!" Emily was friend to both Charlotte and Augusta. The Wilbanks resided in the adjacent property; their home was called Yewhill Grange. "Mama is ever so glad to be rid of us, if only for a few hours, while she's making final preparations to leave."

Charlotte pushed the harp off her shoulder and firmly onto its feet before rising. She straightened the skirts of her green sprig muslin. "Pray, Em, please do not speak of going to Town when Gusta arrives."

"Arrives?" Richard, who had already disposed of his gloves and hat when he entered, glanced about, looking for the eldest sister. "Where is she? I thought she'd meet us at the door with her list of a half-dozen frocks to order from every modiste in Town."

"Oh, such a notion!" Charlotte pressed her fingers to her lips to stifle her giggle.

"And two hats from every milliner, three for each new dress." He directed his discourse first to his sister and then to Charlotte. "Then she'd plan to purchase a reticule for each dress and hat combination."

"That is *famous*!" Charlotte felt her face warm at the idea—extravagance, thy name was Augusta!

"And what other gewgaws does she plan to purchase? I dare not contemplate the possibilities, but I am quite certain she will contrive something as extravagant and outrageous!"

"Oh, Richard," Emily scolded while working off her gloves. "He is truly addled in the upper works, Char-Char. Don't believe a word he says."

Charlotte imagined the finery Augusta would have to do without and felt the smile fade from her face. "But that sounds so delicious—so many dresses, hats, and—"

"What is it, Char-Char?" Emily approached her, seemingly showing as much concern as Charlotte herself felt for her sister.

"Augusta is quite put out because she will miss the beginning of the Season," Charlotte enlightened her friends.

"What?" Emily cried. "You can't mean that!"

"How I wish it were not true, Em. Aunt Penny and

Papa have decided it would be best. They are making plans that she arrive near the end of the Season."

"They think it would be best?" It was difficult to say if Emily was just as upset or more so than Augusta had been. "But how is she ever to meet any gentlemen? They'll all be gone—the good ones will, at any rate."

"One would think as much," Charlotte concurred, but maintained her opinion that her father and her aunt must have known what was best for Augusta—even if she and her sisters, and apparently their friends, had not agreed.

"Where is Gusta now?" Richard seemed genuinely concerned that Augusta was nowhere near.

"She left the breakfast room hours ago. I haven't seen her since." Charlotte moved to the chintz blue-striped sofas near the hearth. "Our tea will be here soon."

"I believe I know where she is to be found. You two need not wait for us." Richard headed for the door. "I'll fetch her."

Augusta glanced down at the rose-colored skirts of her morning dress, then lifted her head to gaze at the marble statue of her mother that stood in the center of the hedge maze. She wished her mother were still alive.

Her mother might have stood in agreement with Papa and Mrs. Parker, but she certainly would have sympathized with Augusta and perhaps taken some of the pain of her disappointment away.

"Gusta, are you all right?"

Augusta spun round at Richard's unexpected voice. "How did you know I was here?" She was not fit company for anyone.

"You always come here when you want to be alone." Richard smiled and tugged at a dry leaf on one of the hedge walls. "I know how upset you must be . . . especially with your father."

"I'm not upset with him in the least." She did her best to look anything but put-out.

Tranquil. Calm. Indifferent.

"I have every confidence that Papa has my best interests at heart. He always has. I have no reason to question him now." But she did not care for his decision.

Richard regarded her beneath his arched eyebrow. "Then what is it that's bothering you?"

"I'm not denying his choice doesn't sit well with me. I had thought . . ."

"Of your mother." The compassion in Richard's voice touched her. "Your mother, if she were still alive, I'm sure would have wholeheartedly agreed with the Duke. You know how famously they got on."

Augusta's parents had been in love. They never argued and above all showed complete devotion to each other and their family.

Richard took up Augusta's hand in a reassuring manner, as he had many times before. "Oh, you shan't miss a thing, I can assure you. Not one dinner party, rout, soiree, or ball will be left to your imagination. I have no doubt that Em will write of every eligible gentleman, if he is worth notice, and he shall be described in excruciating detail—down to the shine on his boots."

"Will she?" Augusta began to feel hopeful that she would not be entirely closed off from news of the Town's festivities.

Oh, what a wonderful friend Emily was.

"I believe it is your father's wish that you be spared the crush of the beginning of the Season." Richard placed her hand on the arm of his brown frock coat and led her away from the statue.

"You mean the fun," Augusta corrected him. Wasn't this what every young lady hoped for—to go to London for the new gowns, to attend parties until all hours of the morning, and to dally with dozens of young men?

"You'll not be missing a thing." Richard stepped away from Augusta. "I can promise you the dramatics will restart when you arrive. Oh, yes!" He chuckled and looked away from her as though he could imagine the scene playing out before him. "Most of the gentlemen, those poor unfortunates who made hasty engagements before your arrival, will consider their futures lost once you arrive. The poor souls who gave up on this Season's finest and have already abandoned Town will rue that decision. Who knows? Some of them may even decide to return."

Augusta giggled at the silly notion.

Richard faced her, his expression all that was serious. "I'm sure there will be more than one young man who'll regret his circumstance once you've made your appearance. Eldest daughter of the Duke of Faraday with a tremendous"—his gaze swept over her—"dowry, a very favorable prospect of a sizeable fortune, as well as an unparalleled beauty. You, my dear Gusta," Richard continued, "are not one to be ignored."

"What was Moo's excuse this time?" Augusta strode into the Blue Parlor as if she were perfectly punctual and anyone who arrived after her should be considered tardy.

She and Richard approached Charlotte and Emily, who were already seated on either side of the tea tray.

"Our dear little sister said she was writing the headmaster, petitioning, yet again, to attend Eton as the first female student," Charlotte answered. "This time she is arguing that her enrollment would illustrate the modern evolution and progressive nature of the establishment."

Richard took the seat next to Emily. Augusta gave an exasperated sigh and sat next to Charlotte, who poured two additional cups for the new arrivals.

"It is simply the most horrid thing, I tell you." Emily's face screwed up in a most unattractive way. "How could it possibly be the best for you? Why would your aunt and father insist Gusta miss the beginning of the Season?"

"Em, will you leave well enough alone!" Richard scolded his sister. "The Duke has made up his mind and I daresay he will not be changing it on your account."

"I can imagine Papa's reasoning very well." Charlotte handed a cup to Richard.

"Do you?" Emily might have been the only other person who understood what Augusta felt.

"If there is a man out there waiting for someone with a fortune, then they would settle on the first lady to come along with a substantial dowry." Charlotte handed a cup to Richard. "It would never occur to them to wait until the end of the Season for our dear Augusta to arrive."

"When one is a fortune hunter, one must secure the fortune at hand." Richard agreed with her.

"Only a man with particular character would wait for just the right woman to come along." Charlotte turned to hand a plate of biscuits to Augusta. "Just as you should wait for the perfect gentleman, my dear sister."

"Must you always be so accommodating?" Augusta snapped, snatching the plate before her. The biscuits nearly slid onto her lap.

"I am sorry if my temperament disturbs you as it is apt to do. There is nothing I can do, for it is my disposition." Sweet-natured Charlotte passed a second plate of small cakes to Emily, who offered them to Richard on her right.

"Do not allow Augusta to vex you, Char-Char." Richard removed one of the cakes for himself. "You are truly an angel and believe me, every man in London will be more than willing to drop at your feet. Perhaps that is what your sister truly fears."

"Oh, dear. I do not want anyone *falling* before me." Charlotte gasped with genuine fright.

"Do not worry, dear, they'll all enjoy it immensely." Richard's smile reassured her.

"Is that not talk you should save for your betrothed?" Augusta couldn't help but dig into Richard's own unfortunate circumstances. He might like everyone to believe he was content with his arranged marriage, but Augusta thought differently. How could one be satisfied with a match not of one's choosing?

"Miss Skeffington and I are well suited, and I am more than willing to proceed with our marriage."

"When will the nuptials take place?" Charlotte appeared greatly interested in Richard's affairs and did not seem to have an adverse opinion of his situation.

"After the Season, I expect. We are allowed our last bit

of freedom before we succumb to the Parson's mouse-trap."

"And how would you compare your Miss Skeffington to . . ." Augusta glanced in Emily's and Charlotte's direction and shrugged. "Let us say, Char-Char?"

Richard glanced over to Augusta's very lovely sister, who blushed attractively at his casual inspection. "I cannot imagine anyone could hold a candle to our delightful Char-Char, but I can with certainty say that Olivia is all that is agreeable."

"How gratifying for you." Augusta displayed a tight smile of her own.

"I count myself a most fortunate man." Richard laid his hand over his heart and bowed his head.

Only time would indeed tell if he were correct.

Time crawled by at a snail's pace. Sitting at Faraday Hall with increased bad humor, Augusta was not to be trifled with. Muriel, whose usual taunts caused arguments that could last for days, found that a mere glance in her elder sister's direction would cause the same outcome. Even Charlotte dared not irritate her older sibling just by being pleasant and polite.

The ensuing absence of Augusta's best friend Emily and her brother Richard did nothing but remind her of how she had been left in the country while they were having a grand time in London.

Emily did not allow a single day to go by without taking up her pen and jotting a lengthy correspondence of the party she attended the night before and the going-ons about Town.

Augusta's cousin Miss Miriam Kimball, also out for

her first Season, wrote her daily. After the end of the third week, Miriam was delighted to announce her engagement to possibly the catch of the Season, Earl Dawson.

Indeed, Augusta felt certain that by the time she arrived in Town, the excitement would have faded, the parties would be thin, and, above all, no single gentlemen would remain.

When the time arrived for her and her aunt to leave, Augusta began to wonder why they should even bother.

Chapter Two

June 1811—London

Augusta and Mrs. Parker arrived in Town three days prior to attending their first assembly. Presently, Augusta rode next to her aunt, across from the Duke, in the Faraday-crested carriage, wearing the most beautiful embroidered white silk gown and matching slippers. A string of pearls intertwined with her auburn hair made a particular striking contrast . . . at least that is what her aunt had told her.

What occupied Augusta's thoughts were the Season's *remainders*—the not-so handsome and not-so young gentlemen who were ignored or refused by other ladies. Upon reflection, she decided the attention of such suitors did not appeal to her in the least.

"Please, Gusta, do try and enjoy yourself," her father chided her. "This is everything you've wished for—your first appearance at Almack's! You will be the toast of the Town before the night is out."

"Your Grace, you are being far too modest," Mrs. Parker amended. Even though they were to attend the as-

14

sembly, her aunt wore a cap and a gray round gown. "I vow there will not be a young man who would not wish to pay court to our dear Gusta."

Augusta felt thankful that neither her aunt nor her father were pressuring her into making a match, and she would do her best to endure the long hours of the evening that stretched out before her.

Her father smiled and his attention moved from his sister-in-law to his daughter. "I was attempting *not* to make her feel more important than she ought."

It had been a very long time since Augusta had seen her father in evening dress. He looked fine enough to make a successful match himself in his white knee breeches, black jacket, snowy white cravat, and black and red striped waistcoat.

The carriage came to a halt. The three occupants alit from the transport and entered the building. They stopped on the first floor landing, entering though the front doors and shedding their outerwear before heading to the main rooms.

"This may not be the most opulent of places, mind. However, nowhere will you find a more notable collection of guests." Augusta's father leaned in closer. "I will caution you to behave yourself."

"I understand, Papa." It was all Augusta could do not to straighten the skirts of her gown or check the condition of her hair. She merely gazed at the brisé fan in her gloved hand and replied, "I realize I am not the angel Charlotte is"—she whispered more softly—"nor am I near as difficult as Moo."

"Rightly so," he agreed, then escorted Augusta through the assembly doors.

The music stopped, leaving silence hanging in the air. The dancers froze mid-step, and the remaining occupants of the brightly lit room came to a standstill.

A hushed ". . . Duke of Faraday" swept through the room, without certainty of origin.

Everyone turned toward them and beheld the Duke of Faraday's eldest daughter. Penny had never seen such a reaction at Almack's.

The orchestra conductor was the first to regain his wits, striking up the musicians and continuing where they had left off. The dancers resumed their progression and the guests returned to their companions. Whispers replaced the normal hums of conversation; the once casual glances grew sharper and more obtrusive.

A woman came toward them. Penny recognized one of the Almack's patronesses, Lady Castlereagh, even though it had been more than a few years since they'd last met.

"Your Grace." Lady Castlereagh bowed her turbaned head and dipped into a curtsy. Her gaze took in not only the Duke but his party. "What an honor to have you join us."

"The pleasure is mine, madam." The Duke turned to Augusta. "May I present Lady Castlereagh? My lady, my daughter Lady Augusta."

Lady Castlereagh's expression showed much interest but very little surprise. "Ah—you are fortunate to have the beauty of the legendary Darling sisters." Her attention drifted from Augusta to Penny.

Augusta's mother, Sarah, and Sarah's two sisters, Mary and Penelope, were renowned for their beauty in their day.

"My dear Duke, Penelope, and my dear niece Augusta—what a delight to see you all." Lady Mary Kimball approached her family. "It has been an age since I've seen you, my beloved sister, and you, Augusta . . . you quite take my breath away. Your cousin Miriam is present and I'm sure the two of you will find ways to amuse yourselves as always. She has spoken of nothing but seeing you this entire day!"

"Allow me to make a few introductions, will you, Your Grace?" Lady Castlereagh interrupted their family reunion, getting back to the business of Almack's, and ushered Augusta away.

Ten minutes later, not one of Augusta's dances remained free.

Augusta gazed upon her dance partner, Sir Albert, and stepped back into the ladies' line, waiting for the music to end. She thanked him and bid him farewell, hoping she'd have more than a few moments to catch her breath before the next set began.

Within the hour of her arrival at Almack's, she had completely changed her mind about coming to Town. Augusta did not know she could enjoy herself this much. The music, the gaiety, and most particularly, the gentlemen were far more enjoyable than she could have imagined.

With her fan in one fist and a handful of her ivory-colored crepe skirt in the other, Augusta's cousin Miriam Kimball rushed to her side.

"You *cannot* dance with Sir Albert Stephenson—he is just engaged to Miss Barbara Leigh this last evening."

"But I have just completed a set with him, Mimi."

Augusta stood very still, wondering if she had made a faux pas. "Is it because he is engaged?"

"He should be dancing with his fiancée," Miriam told Augusta in a scolding tone and sent Sir Albert a dark look across the room.

"Does that mean he cannot dance with any other female?" If that were true Augusta had much to learn. Surely the protocol for such things must be the same here as it was in the country.

"The majority of his time should be spent attending to Miss Leigh, not to you."

"I do apologize." Augusta didn't know what else to say. "Need I express my regrets to Miss Leigh as well?"

"No! Oh, no," Miriam said more quietly and glanced across the way at a very unhappy brunet who sported a delightful band of small white roses in her hair. "That should be even more scandalous."

Augusta sighed. "How is it possible to undo what I have already done?"

"You cannot. There is nothing for it." Miriam exhaled as if all her ministrations and council to her countrified cousin had failed. "I'm afraid there will be talk."

Although quite fond of her cousin, she knew Miriam to love dramatics, and Augusta would not allow herself to become involved. She would *try*, in any case.

"I shan't listen. You cannot possibly blame me for his behavior. I had no idea he was attached to anyone—and I certainly will decline if he should wish another dance."

"Another dance! He cannot help himself, I suppose." Miriam shrugged and added a sigh.

"Cannot help himself? Whatever do you mean?"

"You are a veritable polished jewel compared to

Miss Leigh." Miriam lifted her hand to stop Augusta's next question. "No, no—there is truly no comparison. I daresay he is past regretting their engagement."

"But does he not love her?" Augusta could not imagine how he could dismiss his affection for his new fiancée so easily.

"That is what I've heard." Miriam leaned closer to her cousin to whisper. "His family is in the suds and hers, although not titled, is very wealthy. You see, they complement one another very well. Some may have thought that enough for a successful marriage—and for many it very well would be."

Oh, dear. Perhaps Augusta did have much to learn. She had always believed in friendship and mutual affection, the type of marriage her parents had.

Sir Warren Cantrell, whom Augusta had partnered in her third set, approached with a strikingly handsome gentleman. They stopped before her and bowed.

"Lady Augusta," Sir Warren greeted her. The gentleman accompanying him made a most impressive bow from the waist.

His hair was the color of jet, his eyes a deep blue, and his clothes fit to perfection, displaying his remarkable physique. He quite made the other men of her earlier acquaintance fade from her memory. No hint of a smile played on his handsome countenance, but he continued to regard her in an enticing, somber manner.

"And before I make her known to you, Fieldstone"—Sir Warren edged his companion aside with an elbow—"I wish to claim Lady Augusta for our next set."

"You cannot dance with her *again*," Sir Warren's companion objected.

Augusta *had* already allowed him a second set and had just learned that it was wrong of her.

The gentleman moved forward. "And please show some respect and not kick up dust."

Sir Warren was not to be dissuaded. His eyes brightened and he asked, "Perhaps you would care to join me for a drive tomorrow afternoon? I have a spanking new phaeton with a matched set of grays."

"Well, I am not quite sure . . ." Augusta glanced about, uncertain how she should answer. Perhaps if she were to have some guidance. . . .

"Arrive by three and she may accompany you," Mrs. Parker interjected without missing a beat.

"Oh, splendid! I shall see you at three!" Sir Warren in his highly excitable state dashed off.

"Cantrell, old man!" The dark-haired stranger raised his hand and called after him without success.

"Your lordship," Mrs. Parker interrupted. "If *I* might make my niece known to you."

"I would be most appreciative, ma'am. I thank you." He appeared as if he had forgotten all about Sir Warren and his nonexistent introduction.

Augusta had not taken her gaze from this gentleman since his first word and allowed herself to look up at him more directly.

"Augusta, may I present"—Mrs. Parker receded, allowing them to address one another—"Viscount Fieldstone."

How noble and handsome Lord Fieldstone was! It seemed to Augusta his expression of interest mirrored her own.

"How do you do?" Lord Fieldstone said in a wonderfully sonorous voice.

She extended her gloved hand and allowed her fingertips to rest upon his as she dipped into a curtsy. The momentary silence that rested between them was enough to allow each to draw a slow, single breath.

"May I assume, since Sir Warren is unable to partake of his second dance, it is available?" He leaned toward her as if anticipating a positive response.

"You may, my lord." Augusta could not help but dimple up at him. Oh, she did feel foolish for behaving so missishly, all giggles and smiles.

"I must thank Sir Warren for my good fortune."

"You were my champion, convincing him not to cause a scandal this very evening, were you not?"

"I can see why he might press you to step beyond propriety." Lord Fieldstone openly admired her hair, her dress, then finally her gloved hand, which he continued to hold in his. His face remained unexpressive and his lips never hinted of a smile. "Nor can I disapprove of you for not dancing a second set with him."

"And on my very first evening out. I do have my reputation to consider."

"See there—" He indicated the dance floor, where guests began to line up for the next dance. "Shall we join them?" Lord Fieldstone offered his arm and they headed toward the other guests gathering for the next set.

"Viscount Fieldstone . . . ," Lady Mary Kimball whispered to her younger sister Penny. "That would be a most advantageous match. It is a shame that our dear Sarah is not here to see her eldest daughter make such a success-ful splash."

"Augusta reminds me very much of our sister Sarah. I think she would have been most pleased, Mary," Penny agreed. "They make a most handsome couple, do they not?"

"They certainly do. However, Gusta has only just ar-rived. We have until next week to see what becomes of them," Mary, who Penny always believed knew best, mused. "Nothing, no one, will ever replace her mother, but her aunts will make certain Augusta finds happi-ness."

Chapter Three

Penelope Parker sat in the breakfast room of Worth House enjoying a cup of tea. She could not have been more pleased with her niece's first evening out. What more could Augusta wish for than capturing the attention of every young man in attendance?

A disturbance from the corridor brought Penny to her feet. There would be visitors, to be sure. She had expected there would be some unconventional callers in the days to come . . . but she hadn't counted on ones arriving so early.

Penny headed toward the foyer to see who had arrived. Three young ladies had come to call. Her niece Miriam led the way, followed by her friend Miss Elizabeth Randolph and Augusta's friend Miss Emily Wilbanks.

"Are we too early for a visit?" Miss Randolph appeared uncertain of the etiquette of their impromptu visit.

"Good morning, Mrs. Parker." Emily, who looked very chipper for this hour, was the last to step inside.

The young Miss Wilbanks, whom Penny had watched

mature alongside her sister Sarah's daughters, may not have had the benefit of social connections that position and rank brought, but she came from a well-established family and had a fine education.

"Good day, Aunt Penny." Miriam strode past the butler, Ralston, and untied her bonnet, making it apparent she intended to remain for quite some time. "I told you we would be welcome *anytime*, Lizzie, you goose."

Penny added, to her previous thoughts, that sometimes Emily behaved *better* than her own relatives. "Keeping country hours, are you?" she teased, knowing very well Augusta's best friend wanted to hear news of Almack's since she could not attend.

"Look at all these flowers!" Emily exclaimed, glancing about but coming to settle on a card protruding from a bunch of violets.

"Lady Augusta could not have *danced* with this many men," Lizzie, who had also not attended Almack's the previous evening, commented, sounding wary.

"She did make the acquaintance of many more gentlemen than she shared dances." Miriam handed her bonnet to Penny, as free space on the table was nonexistent.

"Do you mean to tell me that some men sent tributes without the benefit of a dance?" Emily remarked, quite shocked at the very idea.

"It must be so. How else can you account for such a display?" Miriam gestured to the collection of flowers lining every flat surface in the marble entryway and extending into the front cerulean blue parlor.

"If you young ladies would wait for Augusta in the breakfast room. She has not yet come belowstairs but I expect her soon." Penny led the way. Once they had arrived, she motioned to the sideboard. "Please help yourselves—tea, chocolate, coffee, if you like."

"Thank you." Emily poured herself tea.

"I daresay callers will be arriving in a few hours' time," Lizzie voiced, sounding excited.

"Gusta had best be ready for the day." Emily moved around the breakfast table and seated herself.

"And she is to go out for a drive at three," Miriam informed her, "with Sir Warren."

"Cantrell?" Emily guessed hopefully and then sighed, perhaps a bit envious of her best friend's success. "What a wonderful evening Gusta must have had!"

"One might have thought such, but I believe she was determined not to enjoy herself when she arrived." Miriam poured a cup of chocolate for Lizzie, then herself.

"Fustian!" Lizzie cried. "It was her first assembly."

"And was it not Almack's?" Emily tilted her head as if she wondered that she had somehow misunderstood.

Penny knew Emily did not need to attend to know her friend's mind. Those two understood one another very well.

"Our dear Gusta did not want for partners—there was a line of men just waiting to have a chance." Miriam punctuated her words with a significant nod of her head. "You should have seen them, Em. All of them lined up for Gusta's attention, all of them clamoring to be the first to partner her. I believe she must have crushed the hopes of no less than three dozen gentlemen last night."

"Good gracious, Miriam—honestly," Augusta snapped from the doorway.

"Good morning, Gusta," Emily greeted cheerfully.

"It is very nice to see *you*, Em," Augusta acknowledged. "I suggest you only listen to half of what my cousin says and ignore the other half."

Miriam huffed. "I beg you to speak to my aunt. She was there and saw what truly happened."

"I shall leave you girls to your gossip." Aunt Penny diplomatically avoided the conversation, as she was known to do in the Faraday household. "I'm going to take the carriage to call on your mother, Miriam, to see if she could use any help for her party this evening."

A ball, given in Augusta's honor by her aunt Mary, had been planned many weeks ago, as it was known the Season would be over soon.

"Please tell her I am looking forward to this evening." Augusta stepped into the room.

"Certainly, my dear." Aunt Penny made her exit.

The four girls waited patiently until they were certain Mrs. Parker was well out of hearing range before continuing their discussion.

"I had a splendid time," Augusta stated, directly to Emily, "and there were exactly the number of gentlemen I needed to dance every set and no more than that."

"I am quite sure that long before you made the acquaintance of Lord Fieldstone, you must have decided all was going quite well." Lizzie said, and then added, "I certainly would have."

"I believe it must have begun, if I am not mistaken, with Sir Albert's insistence that he claim your first dance." Miriam lifted her cup and saucer from the table. "There was some *heated* discussion among the young bloods."

Augusta faced the sideboard and groaned with exasperation. Why did Miriam feel the need to overexaggerate at every occasion?

"One's opinion of any gathering always improves when there are gentlemen battling over you," Miriam declared over the rim of her cup. "However, Sir Albert managed to prevail!"

"Is *that* why Sir Albert Stephenson has begged off?" Lizzie leaned forward, nearly spilling her chocolate.

"He's broken his engagement to Miss Leigh? The scoundrel!" Emily remarked with her eyes wide with outrage.

"I told you not to dance with him!" Miriam scolded Augusta and then turned to face her friend. "Pray, how do you know this?"

"I have had it from my abigail Marybelle," Lizzie replied.

"So that bit of news must be true if you got it from your lady's maid." Augusta would not allow herself to be manipulated by servants' gossip. She poured a portion of milk into a Meissen china cup before dispensing her tea.

"It's not just the servants, Augusta. I heard Mama tell Papa the very same this morning before I left." Lizzie steadied her cup and its contents.

"And where do you think your mother got her information?" Augusta asked her, all the while knowing what the answer would be.

Lizzie blinked and twirled a strand of her hair around her finger, considering the question. "I don't know exactly. I suppose she must have heard it or been told by one of the . . . servants."

"You see." Augusta leveled a stern look at the trio. "It is just as I said. Until we hear from Miss Leigh or her family we cannot assume this hearsay is true."

"That is not the way things are done in Town, Gusta!" Miriam reprimanded her cousin in a tone that told her she was being childish. Augusta somehow endured Miriam's need to play a maternal role to her younger cousin of only two months.

"Do you mean to tell me that we are to believe every servant's tale?" Augusta furrowed her brows at Miriam, who looked quite taken aback. "Is that how we go about—believing every thread of gossip?"

"It is knowledge to forewarn us. We do not wish to appear foolish, do we?" she returned with equal temper. "To not know what is going on about us is far worse than having to *pretend* we do not know."

Augusta turned to catch Emily's and Lizzie's reaction to Miriam's pronouncement.

"I consider Sir Albert completely unsuitable. I shan't receive him." Augusta pushed a bouquet of flowers aside, refusing to acknowledge their presence, as if they embodied Sir Albert himself. "He will be barred from entering the house should he dare to call."

"I'm afraid he might dare," was Emily's timid reply. "Richard told me he had heard Sir Albert felt compelled to seek out your favor."

"The *roué*!" Miriam must have found Sir Albert's action as repulsive as Augusta had. "How could he think you'd accept him after breaking his engagement to Miss Leigh?"

"I cannot possibly forgive him—that odious fortune hunter!" Augusta agreed. "And speaking of Richard, where has he been keeping himself? In Miss Skeffington's pocket, I presume."

"Where else?"

"Are they to wed at last?" Miriam set her cup and saucer on the table.

"Their marriage was arranged long ago, but it was Richard's wish that Olivia enjoy a Season before they marry," Emily told Miriam and Lizzie.

"I think that is very considerate of him." Augusta knew Richard to be a fair, dutiful, and indisputably reliable person. "We should all do well to find a gentleman as thoughtful as your brother."

"But Gusta, you are so fortunate to have so many admirers." Emily motioned to the flowers lining the room. "I'm quite sure each and every gentleman would do what they must to gain your favor."

"Your family connection alone is—"

"Please, Miriam, Gusta is not here to find a business associate but her heart," Emily interrupted. Thankfully she completely understood Augusta's predicament.

"And how should I ever make such a momentous decision as that by the end of the Season? That comes in less than one week's time."

Although she had only attended a single function, Augusta could imagine the complications if there were a repeat of last night—too many gentlemen and so little time.

"Lord Fieldstone is only one of many gentlemen seeking your attention," Miriam reminded her cousin. "It is well enough to cross Sir Albert off your list to make room for others."

The others. The thought of all those gentlemen, with

the exception of Sir Albert, made Augusta feel a bit humbled. Was she truly worthy of all this attention?

"What's wrong, Gusta?" Miriam teased. "Do you not think you can manage this many men?"

Augusta felt her face warm and resisted pressing her cheeks. She would not give her cousin the satisfaction of seeing her do so.

"I should like to try." Lizzie grinned.

"Oh, Lizzie, you are shameful!" Miriam giggled.

"Just a bit, and only very infrequently," Lizzie admitted, with her smile taking on a naughty air.

"I will agree that Lord Fieldstone has a great deal to recommend him." Surely Augusta could not make such an important decision in the matter of a few days. "It may come to pass that we do not suit."

"Not suit? Are you mad?" Miriam nearly jumped out of her seat. "Who would ever think not to consider his suit?"

"I never said a word about refusing him." Augusta remained calm, hoping her demeanor would keep her cousin so. "I am merely taking each day and each event as it comes. Despite my initial impressions of what I would find when I came to Town, it seems I am quite enjoying myself . . . the dancing and the gentlemen's attentions . . . and I cannot see why I cannot continue to do so. Matrimony, at this time, is not my primary concern."

That evening, after the second dance set of the Kimball ball, Augusta stood to one side of the dance floor watching the sparkling reflections from crystal chandeliers hanging high above the rented hall. Still catching her breath from the last dance, she took a few moments to savor the sounds of the guests moving about and the murmurs of their conversations that filled the room.

She felt beautiful in her fine white striped muslin gown with its shimmering overskirt, her hair styled just so with cascading curls framing her face, and her mother's gold locket around her neck. Augusta fully intended to enjoy herself this night.

Aunt Penny had told Augusta they would be attending a small dinner party tomorrow night, then next week a musical soiree. Augusta could also count on another drive through the park with Sir Warren. That he had promised her this very evening. Then there were gentlemen callers—plentiful enough—but there was something unpleasant about all those men wanting her attention all at the same time . . . well, it was impossible!

"Does one ever tire of hearing how charming or how lovely one is?" Emily laughed, coming upon Augusta. "I enjoy the attention, as do you, I am quite sure."

Augusta had just finished a set with Lord Carlton Wingate, and had, before the music began, made the acquaintance of Lord Andrews. Lord Andrews seemed to be a kindly elderly man. She guessed him to be much older than her father.

"Oh, look, Gusta—see who approaches." Emily dropped her fan open and fluttered it, cooling them both.

Augusta turned. "Lord Fieldstone, how delightful to see you again!" She had to admit that she was flattered by his interest. And oh, how serious he appeared.

He made one of his from-the-waist bows, which made her feel very special indeed. "I had stopped by to call this afternoon but never made it to the front door. What a crush of callers you had!"

"I'm afraid there were far too many. I am so sorry to have missed you."

"Perhaps if I were to come another time, say a bit earlier . . . tomorrow at eleven or better yet . . . ten in the morning," he suggested and ventured further by proposing, "I could escort you and your aunt on a shopping expedition?"

How considerate he was to offer.

"And I would, of course, have you home in time to receive your other callers."

"That sounds splendid. I shall look forward to your visit, as should my aunt, I expect."

"Until tomorrow, then." With a second delicious bow he retreated. Augusta watched him leave through the main doors. There, entering the room, she noticed a particular gentleman.

For shame, she thought, how easily her head turned when a handsome young man was about.

The color of his hair and the shape of his face were familiar to her. She stood across the room, much too far away to guess his identity.

Certainly he was well-dressed, as were all the males in attendance . . . tall . . . and quite handsome—oh, dear . . . Augusta looked closer to see if it was indeed who she thought it was—Richard . . . Richard Wilbanks?

She could hardly believe how grown he appeared, how quite handsome, and now, he headed in her direction.

"Come now, Gusta," Richard said to her when he

arrived. "You will certainly not take if you present this Friday-faced dowd to the *ton.*"

"Richard, you are being rude," Emily scolded.

The sight of him dressed in a splendidly tailored black coat and trousers took her breath away. Never had he looked so grown. He stood before her not as the young lad she had always thought of but as a man.

"You should be kind to her," his sister urged. "Say something nice. Something that will make her feel wonderful and pretty."

"Gusta!" Richard nearly shouted, for Augusta was not paying attention to him.

"I beg your pardon?" What had he said to her?

"Do you perchance have a dance available?" he asked, attempting to keep the begrudging tone from his query, without success. "Emily insists we share a dance."

She didn't have to check. Augusta knew she did not have a dance available. "I'm sorry. Perhaps if you would have asked earlier."

"Ah, you see?" He leaned close and whispered. "You are the ever-lovely Char-Char's sister, are you not? These men, too, will soon be falling at your feet." He stepped back and gave a slight bow. "It is my misfortune, then. Perhaps next time?"

"Next time, sir." Augusta dipped into a shallow curtsy and watched him leave.

"Sir? Gusta, that is *Richard."* Emily prodded her with the end of her fan.

"Yes, I know it is Richard. I've just never seen him so . . . so . . ." Augusta stared in his direction, thinking . . . thinking nothing in particular, merely gazing at his retreating form.

"He was only trying to be polite. He's now about to inquire after Miss Skeffington. See her there, standing with her mother and your aunt Lady Kimball?"

Miss Olivia Skeffington seemed quite pretty. She swept the skirts of her peach-colored gown aside to address her intended when he approached. If she possessed in manners what she possessed in beauty, Richard would be a very lucky man indeed. And above all, Augusta did want to see her friend happy.

Richard returned with Miss Skeffington's arm draped through his. "Miss Skeffington wishes to pay her regards."

"How nice it is to see you again," Augusta said to Richard's lady.

"It has been a very long time. We were mere children the last we met." Miss Skeffington's blue eyes widened as if in shock. "You are quite grown and even more lovely than I recall. Why, Richard, you never told me she was so beautiful."

"I—I—" he stammered, clearly caught off guard. He stared at Augusta as if he had been caught admiring her.

"You are going to ask her to dance, are you not?" Miss Skeffington prompted.

"Emily has already had me inquire," he supplied. "Unfortunately, Lady Augusta is occupied for the entire evening—and if I am not mistaken, happily so."

Yes, Augusta was quite pleased to take part in every set.

"I should not think it improper for you to dance with her at all," Miss Skeffington continued. "Why, I would think dancing with her should be nearly the same as sharing a dance with your own sister."

"Perhaps next time I will prove more fortunate. Shall *we*, my dear?" He pivoted to lead her away. "If you will excuse us, ladies?"

In another moment Emily's dance partner arrived and Lord Perkins claimed his dance with Augusta. Standing in the ladies' line across from him, she could not suppress the strange mixture of dissatisfaction and envy that rose within her.

The musical interlude began and couples moved onto the floor, Richard and Miss Skeffington among them. Augusta glimpsed them step around one another as they came together in the steps of the dance. The couple gazed upon one another comfortably, their mouths moving in pleasant conversation. The private, shy smiles they shared should not have been observed by anyone.

"I say, Lady Augusta . . . ," Lord Perkins addressed her, but his words passed unnoticed.

Augusta fully realized she should pay attention but simply could not. Something unwanted and unexpected filled her while watching Richard and Miss Skeffington.

It was of no consequence to Augusta that she had missed out on the majority of this Season's festivities. She had no true interest in finding a husband and marrying. None of it had mattered until this very moment.

Now that she had seen Richard and Miss Skeffington . . . the sight of them together, sharing pleasant, amiable company, displayed to Augusta exactly what it was she desired.

At that moment Augusta knew what she must do. She needed to find a husband. A suitable husband whose company she could enjoy and a man who could make her feel comfortable and fully at ease.

She blinked up at the very handsome, delightfully charming Lord Perkins and imagined how it would feel if she were in love with him.

Augusta hadn't felt any such thing but wished the emotion would rise within her. Then she wondered if it would with any of the men she'd met. Her gaze swept the room for the gentlemen with whom she'd recently become acquainted.

Without meaning to she had, in manner of course, made somewhat of a personal list of eligibles, even ranked them in order of preference. How could she prevent doing so with Emily, Lizzie, and Miriam weighing the merit and measure of every man Augusta met?

Augusta would make this secret list of gentlemen, keep it to herself, and with it she would search among them for her husband.

Chapter Four

Not only had Lord Fieldstone proved to be a splendid companion, he spared no expense spoiling Augusta and her aunt during the next morning's shopping expedition. Aunt Penny would not allow him to purchase a dashing straw-chip bonnet for Augusta. However, he managed to procure the green ribbon and silk flowers for its embellishment, and made her promise to give him an opportunity to view the results when she had finished decorating her hat.

An outcome Augusta found very promising indeed.

Upon their return to Worth House, Lord Fieldstone bid them both a fond adieu and sketched a bow before taking his leave. Augusta saw him to the door herself. She leaned against the open portal and tugged at the fingers of her gloves, removing them. She watched the Viscount move down the front steps, admiring the fit of his trousers and the precise cut of his coat with his departure.

No sooner had Lord Fieldstone turned from the

house than Emily, Lizzie, and cousin Miriam came up the front walk.

He paused and stepped to one side, allowing them to pass. He tipped his hat and acknowledged them with "Ladies . . ."

At the baritone timbre of his voice, an expression of rapture spread across their faces and, most probably, weakened their knees beneath their fashionable walking gowns.

"That was Viscount Fieldstone!" Lizzie said in a voice that must have echoed off every residence of Hanover Square. "Augusta is so very lucky that he has shown interest in her."

Augusta might have felt self-conscious about the proclamation if it hadn't been true. She wasn't sure that shouting in the middle of Town would have been her method of alerting the inhabitants of the news.

Augusta drew them into the house by their arms, skirts, sleeves, reticules—whatever she managed to get ahold of—and closed the door.

Emily pressed her hand to her lips but she was far from managing to suppress her laughter.

Miriam's gaze slid to Augusta before commenting, "Did you not think Gusta and Lord Fieldstone were the most handsome couple on the floor last night?"

Emily closed her eyes and allowed her held breath to escape with a sigh. "I have heard that he has managed to successfully evade the marriage mart, holding out for his perfect bride!"

"Lady Augusta, that could be you!" Lizzie shrilled.

Fieldstone's viscountess? Even Augusta thought it too soon to travel down that path. After giving the subject a few moments of consideration, the notion had some appeal, and she could not deny her attraction to him.

Lord Fieldstone was most impressive—handsome, well-mannered, and well-spoken. He could easily walk away with Augusta's heart if she were to permit it. However, there were other gentlemen to consider before she needed to choose a husband—and besides, he had yet to ask her.

If the decision were left to Miriam, Lizzie, and Emily, Lord Fieldstone was the most desirable and he would be the man Augusta would marry.

Augusta might have agreed with them, but it was impossible for her to know if he were her choice until they were better acquainted. She did not wish to wed a complete stranger.

How circumstances had changed. Miriam, Lizzie, and Emily gossiped and giggled while Augusta felt the full importance of her presence in Town. It was not to strictly enjoy herself but to engage a gentleman through her flirtations. She needed to attract the right sort of gentleman, one who would make an ideal husband. All of a sudden she felt her girlish silliness fall by the wayside, replaced by the notion that she was quite grown up.

Emily, Lizzie, and Miriam brought Augusta near, into their confidential coze to discuss the recent gossip they'd heard last night and that very morning from their servants.

Augusta listened to how Miss Constance Greenfield-Jones tried to catch the eye of the obscenely rich Lord Arthur Masters and how Lord Crandall had begged off his engagement to the lovely Lady Catherine Willows, who, by his estimation, was not as lovely as Lady Augusta Worth. He gave the excuse that he could not, in good conscience, shackle himself to her without first offering himself for judgment to the Duke of Faraday's daughter.

As if Augusta could be tempted by such a blackguard. And if Lady Catherine possessed any self-respect or the smallest amount of activity under her bonnet, she would not even acknowledge him when he returned to beg her forgiveness. Such behavior was not to be borne.

Augusta wasn't sure how long this grown-up-Augusta would last, but the fun and frivolity of the girl-Augusta seemed to ebb. She now felt quite serious in her pursuit of a suitable man.

How she wished that she, too, could still believe life could remain all fun and frolic.

That evening, Augusta, her cousin Miriam, and Mrs. Parker attended a dinner party at Lord and Lady Sutherland's. Apparently, Lady Sutherland thought that Augusta's attendance would ensure a number of eligible gentlemen for her own unattached daughter, Miss Emma Sutherland.

Far more males than females attended, which appeared a bit odd especially if one considered that Augusta's cousin Miriam and Earl Dawson were already engaged. The remaining gentlemen fell all over themselves competing for time with the remaining two unattached young ladies. Correction: they made absolute cakes of themselves vying for Augusta's attention and ignoring Miss Sutherland altogether.

At the conclusion of supper, Mr. Bertram Allendale apparently had no interest in remaining with the gentlemen for an after-dinner port and turned to his right. "I hear tell that the Sutherlands have a fine gallery, Lady Augusta. Would you care to take a turn?"

Sir Benjamin Palfrey shot to his feet and tugged his waistcoat taut, moving toward the head of the table where Augusta sat. "Yes, I beg you to allow me to escort you, Lady Augusta."

"Might we *all* be allowed to share in Lady Augusta's company?" Lord Carlton huffed, sounding wholly unsatisfied that mention of the other guests had been omitted.

"I shall need an escort"—Mrs. Parker glanced from one side of her to the other, looking for gentlemen to volunteer, and offering them kind smiles if they were to oblige—"or two."

"I would be delighted, Mrs. Parker. If you would do me the honor?" A dashing Lord Stanton stood and helped her from her seat. Lord Carlton Wingate reluctantly accepted and took her other arm.

"Oh, I say *this* is far more agreeable than lying about the dining room partaking spirits without the enjoyment of the ladies' company," Lord Carlton enunciated in a rather loudish manner.

Augusta had heard him but was already in conversation with the two men on either side of her. Sir Benjamin wasted no time and offered to accompany her for an afternoon visit to Kew Gardens. She was delighted to accept.

No sooner had she agreed to Sir Benjamin's afternoon

diversion than Mr. Allendale, who would not be outdone, suggested she might care for a far more adventurous journey—a trip to the Exeter Exchange!

Cousin Miriam's fiancé, Earl Dawson, happily escorted her, and Sir Samuel Pruitt offered her his arm as well. The remaining two gentlemen, Lord Perkins and Lord Bancroft, escorted Miss Emma Sutherland. The four groups of three headed out of the dining room for their stroll through the gallery.

The next afternoon, Penny could not keep Miriam, Lizzie, and Emily from peering out the double-sash windows facing the front of Worth House. They stood on tiptoes, watching for Augusta to return from her drive in Sir Warren's green high-perched phaeton.

Penny approached the girls. "Come away from there." They huddled closer and appeared completely intrigued with the arrival of the vehicle rolling up the street.

"Watch out, they'll see us!" Miriam cried out.

Penny drew the three away. "Into the parlor, we shall wait for Gusta there." She urged the girls down the corridor but she could not resist a quick glance out the window herself before following them.

"Is Sir Warren not handsome?" Miriam looked to Lizzie and Emily for their thoughts. "I think he must find Gusta very agreeable. This is her second drive with him in his new phaeton."

"Do you think she cares for him as well?" Lizzie wondered.

"I'm afraid I would be terrified out of my wits to climb aboard such a vehicle," Emily confessed, sounding timid. "It is very high."

"But he is ever so handsome."

"Miriam, I am not about to marry anyone because he is handsome," Emily remarked in a stern tone.

"Nor would I turn one away because he owns a high-perched transport," Lizzie confessed.

"I thank you for your company, Lady Augusta," Sir Warren's voice echoed in from the marble entryway. "Might we share another drive through the park in a few days?"

The occupants of the cerulean blue parlor went quiet as they waited for Augusta's answer. There was a reply but much too soft for any of them to decipher.

"Very well, then," he said. The answer must not have been the one he wanted. "Until we meet again—and I pray that it may be soon. Good day to you."

Penny and the girls all looked at one another wide-eyed, completely silent, still, waiting for something to—

Augusta strolled into the room, extremely slowly. When she saw them perched upon the sofa unnaturally motionless, she inquired, "What are you lot doing?"

"We did not wish to disturb you." Penny seemed to be quite shocked at Augusta's somber demeanor.

"I . . . I need to sit . . . ," Augusta began, ". . . on something that does not move."

Miriam, Lizzie, and Emily giggled.

"And someplace where my feet can touch the solid floor."

Miriam and Emily laughed again.

"Let me fetch you some tea, dear. You don't look very well at all." Penny stood and headed out the door.

"Thank you, Aunt Penny," Augusta called after her.

"What happened? Was it thrilling?" Emily's excitement could not be contained.

"Is he as famous a whip as I have heard?" Lizzie begged her to answer.

Augusta managed to look at her best friend, but she quite felt that her expression might have given away her lackluster opinion. "I really can't speak of it now. I need to recover from the ordeal."

Emily gasped. "Oh, dear."

"And while we wait, Em"—Miriam turned to her left—"allow me to tell you and Lizzie what happened after dinner at the Sutherland's last night."

"Oh, yes, do tell us, Mimi." Lizzie shifted so as to look squarely upon the speaker.

"After dinner we all lined up, three abreast—two men for each female, one on each of the ladies' arms—and we made our way down through the long gallery."

"So the men outnumbered the women? Was that not awkward? Were not some of the men left out?" Emily wanted to know, and she leaned forward, showing great interest.

"Actually, some of the women"—Miriam turned toward Emily and whispered—"Miss Sutherland, poor dear"—then spoke at her normal volume—"did not manage to engage any of the gentlemen."

That wasn't entirely true but Augusta felt too out of sorts to correct her cousin.

"You should have seen Lord Carlton." Miriam glanced heavenward and exhaled, displaying her full exasperation. "He nearly came to tears when he could not take Gusta's arm on our return trip through Sutherland's gallery."

August had to speak up. "The gentlemen insisted that . . ." How was she to explain without sounding conceited?

There was no need, for Miriam continued, "The ladies had to exchange gentlemen escorts once we'd arrived and there were some who nearly came to blows—for there were seven eligible gentlemen, and Augusta was limited to two arms. She could not accommodate them all."

Lizzie let out a cry of laughter while Emily tried to stifle hers.

"It was not as horrible as that." Augusta tried to downplay the event, but even she had to admit that it was a truly frightening scene—and she was enormously relieved it had not come down to fisticuffs.

"I believe I did see Lord Carlton's eyes welling up with tears during our return to the drawing room when Gusta announced that she could not accept any more offers for afternoon outings. She said they were all welcome to call, when it was convenient for them, and she would be most delighted to see them *if* they were to catch her at home."

There was a knock at the open door before Ralston entered and offered her a card upon a salver. "Pardon me, Lady Augusta, Sir Samuel Pruitt has arrived. Shall I show him in?"

"No, I'll—" Augusta thought it best she shield Sir Samuel from the prying eyes of her friends, or perhaps worse, their gossiping tongues.

"Excuse me." Augusta rose and stood for a moment to make certain she could stand upright without losing her balance. She headed out the door, turned to the right, and walked down the corridor.

"Lady Augusta—" Sir Samuel stood just beyond Mrs. Parker in the marble entryway with his hat and walking stick in hand. "I feared I would be denied the pleasure of calling on you this afternoon, so I thought I might chance an intrusion by stopping by a bit early." He made a shallow bow. "Mrs. Parker tells me you are—" Sir Samuel stepped forward and spoke very softly. "I can see for myself that you look a bit pale." His eyes narrowed and he observed her with a tilt of his head. "You do not seem as if you are feeling the thing."

"I believe I need—" Augusta wasn't quite sure what she needed, but no, she did not feel *the thing* at all.

Today's drive, unquestionably, had not agreed with her.

She wasn't sure which put her off the most, the precarious height of the phaeton or the baronet attempting to break a land record of a particular peer's, accounting for today's accelerated speed.

"Was it Sir Warren and that ridiculous green monstrosity of his?" Sir Samuel guessed, raising one of his well-formed eyebrows, but he did not wait for her to answer and continued, "It is obvious you have been through somewhat of a shock. Your nerves are quite overwrought." He paused. "Might I suggest something . . . more soothing, calming?"

She glanced at her aunt, who had stepped back from the couple out of sight, just around the corner. Augusta did not need to wonder how much her relative had heard. She guessed her aunt had witnessed *everything*.

"A stroll through a lovely garden, perhaps?" He watched Augusta's reaction as if to measure her approval. "If I may, I will take you to a place where there are beautiful, exquisite flowers to gaze upon. It will remind you of your sorely missed gardens at Faraday Hall."

Truly, could he do such a thing in the middle of Town?

"It shall restore you and you'll feel quite . . . transported, I promise you." A wondrous smile crossed his face that convinced her that every word he spoke was to be believed.

Augusta found herself returning his sentiment. Her glance to her aunt did not go unnoticed by Sir Samuel. He stepped to Mrs. Parker's side and they had a short, quiet conversation. She smiled and apparently gave her consent to whatever it was he had proposed.

"We shall return shortly, and do not fear, I shall not allow any harm to come to her." Sir Samuel returned to Augusta with a renewed bounce in his step and offered her his arm.

The man was so impatient, honestly, he had to be reminded that Augusta needed to collect her bonnet and pelisse before leaving. They stepped outside onto the walk.

"We need only travel down the street here and turn left." Sir Samuel gestured with his hat before replacing it upon his head. "My aunt lives down only a few houses more."

Not that Augusta found walking distasteful, but it really was not conducive to eliminating the pain in her head. Sir Samuel did seem empathetic to her discomfort and reassured her that with the short stroll and their engaging conversation, they would arrive in no time at all.

"We hardly had a chance to speak last night," he reminded her, then chuckled. "Not that there was enough time. You had more than your fair share of admirers."

"I do apologize." Augusta remembered he had attended the Sutherland dinner. He sat where it was impossible for them to speak, and she could barely see him throughout the duration of the meal.

"There is nothing for it." He shrugged. "Can't imagine what you could have done any differently. Ah—here we are now." Sir Samuel motioned to an arched opening with a tall, sturdy iron gate.

Ivy, originating from beyond the gate, clung to the building. The greenery seemed to creep out and around from the outer edges, toward the street, softening the starkness of the smooth surface.

"We'll go in through the side entrance." He fished about in his vest pocket and pulled out a key. "We'll let ourselves in, the Baroness won't mind." With a well-practiced turn, the deed was done and moments later the iron gate swung open.

"Is she at home?" Augusta took a tentative step into the lush green courtyard.

"I believe so. One can usually find her tending her garden."

Augusta's gaze came to rest upon a person wearing a large hat, who squatted low to the ground tending to the plants, and who was seemingly unaware of the creak of the gate as they entered.

"Samuel, have you returned so soon?" The gardener did not stand or glance in their direction.

"Aunt, I have brought a guest," Sir Samuel announced.

"Without any warning?" The hat came off with one hand; in the other were a pair of clippers that disappeared into an apron pocket. The woman turned to regard them.

"Look at me—I'm in no condition to receive guests." She pulled at her gloves, removing them, and brushed at the skirt of her hopelessly soiled apron. "I daresay I believed you had better manners than that."

There was no shame in her partaking of her hobby in the privacy of her home. Augusta wished the Baroness would not feel as if she had done something improper.

"Lady Augusta, will you allow me to present my aunt, the Dowager Baroness Vernon?" Sir Samuel motioned to the woman who resembled a gardener. "Lady Augusta is feeling poorly and I suggested she stroll through your magnificent garden and see if it does not set her to feeling right once again."

"Might I suggest you head toward the kitchen corner? It's at the far end, and just to the right," Lady Vernon said. "That particular spot does wonders for easing one's mind. Just continue down that path."

Sir Samuel walked Augusta forward and urged her to move on at her own pace.

"Thank you." Augusta stepped in the indicated direction, hesitating long enough to hear the woman call out to her.

"If you will be so kind as to excuse me, I will take this time to change out of these work clothes into something more appropriate."

"I shall be fine, my lady." Augusta reassured her. She released Sir Samuel's arm, indicating that she would venture off on her own.

Lady Vernon whispered to her nephew, "Samuel, would you be so good as to inform Mrs. Crumb that I would like a tea tray brought out for us?"

Augusta glanced back to see the two of them soon leave the garden and disappear into the house. She continued her stroll toward the kitchen corner as directed.

Augusta had taken only a few steps into the garden before she felt immeasurably better. The cooling breeze, the delightful floral scents, the beautiful flowers surrounding her . . .

This garden, lying behind the townhouse . . . it should have been shady—but somehow the sun filtered down to the plants that appeared to be perfectly content and thriving in their various pots and planters.

A single white tulip sat among the twenty red ones, growing in a rectangular container. A dozen pink hollyhocks stood erect in the corner flanked by two enormous ferns.

She passed pink and white roses mingling with delphiniums that must have hid one wall. Lobelia tumbled out of pots, covering the feet of the long spiked flowers of mignonette.

Augusta began to feel as if she were truly walking down a path in the country. She glanced to her left and saw . . .

"Are those really bluebells?" A flower so familiar to her, it brought to mind the woods near Faraday Hall, the path she would take to visit the Wilbankses at Yewhill Grange. The tall, thin trees with their new spring leaves so very green, and the dense carpet of bluebells at their roots . . . but this was not spring and this was London, not the country.

The scent of mint drifted in the air before her, tempting her to continue to find its source. By the time Augusta came upon the profusion of mint that scented the air, she noticed planted nearby the many sprigs of parsley and the woody stalks of the massive fragrant rosemary bush among the so very many other herbs that would be employed by the kitchen.

"How are you feeling?" Lady Vernon, approaching from the house, looked distinguished in a modest cap and lilac morning dress.

"I feel as if I have been walking in the country for hours." Augusta wondered exactly how much time had passed.

"It hasn't been as long as that." The Baroness chuckled. "There is a tea tray on the veranda table. Will you join me?"

"I have arrived unannounced. I do not wish to take up more of your afternoon than I already have." Augusta walked alongside the Baroness.

"Nonsense. You are already here and the tea is waiting. Please let us sit." Lady Vernon gestured toward the small round table with a sweep of her arm.

"Very well." Augusta moved toward the table, taking the chair that faced the flowers. "You do have a most amazing garden, Lady Vernon, with almost magical healing qualities."

They both laughed. The corner of the Baroness's eyes crinkled when she smiled. She had the most kind-hearted manner about her, making conversation easy and her company enjoyable.

"Do you take sugar in your tea?"

"No, thank you." Augusta looked around, wondering about Sir Samuel's whereabouts. "Will your nephew not be joining us?"

"He has indicated that you are not to have tea without

some sort of exquisite tidbits from a certain confectionary shop—of which the name completely escapes me." Lady Vernon laughed at herself and poured a bit of milk into each cup before pouring the tea. "He has gone to fetch them himself. I have every confidence he shall return shortly."

"He shouldn't have gone to the bother." Augusta could not imagine what had possessed him to deposit her with his aunt and dash out for biscuits, no matter how delectable.

"Are you certain you are feeling quite well?" The Baroness handed Augusta her cup and saucer.

"I am—as Sir Samuel put it—*transported*. I assure you." She sipped from the cup.

"I do not mean to pry, but it has come to my notice that my nephew holds you in great esteem. He has spoken quite highly of you."

"I cannot imagine what he could say. We only met at the Sutherland's last night. And, unfortunately, we were not able to converse."

"Ah, so you do not know much about him." The casual comment sounded anything but.

"I'm afraid not." Augusta wondered what it was she should know about him.

"He is the eldest son of the Earl of Hampstead, grandson of the Duke of Cubberleigh, and is in line to inherit both titles. He has two younger brothers, and a younger sister."

"I am the eldest of three sisters, and I have a younger brother."

Lady Vernon chuckled. "He understands that he will

become duke one day and wishes to conduct himself accordingly—to marry someone who will be a suitable duchess." She glanced at Augusta from the corner of her eye. "Before this morning he had not even mentioned any young lady of interest."

"If by that you mean that he has taken notice of me . . . all I can say is . . . I am deeply flattered." Augusta considered that Sir Samuel might very well be vying with Lord Fieldstone for the top of her list.

"I would expect the daughter of a duke to be much more forthright. At least as self-assured as a young man who will come into such a title." Lady Vernon paused to draw in a measured breath. "I do have one small reservation."

Did the Baroness consider her family unsuitable? Or their connections perhaps? Could she have an objection to Augusta herself? She had been in Town not even a week; even she needed more time than that to tarnish her reputation.

Augusta had thought she and the Baroness were getting along splendidly—only now to discover that Lady Vernon did not like her at all?

"Do not mistake me, it is not you I have my doubts about. It is Samuel."

"Sir Samuel has been all that is kind. I assure you my aunt would never have permitted me to leave the house with him unless his character was above reproach."

"Yes, I completely agree." Lady Vernon's face relaxed, and Augusta got the feeling that this might not be as serious as she had first feared. "I understand how you might agree my nephew is suitable *parti*. He is handsome, intelligent, and very considerate—especially to those of whom he is fond. All characteristics a woman would wish in a husband."

Then what was the difficulty? Augusta had no idea. She looked upon Lady Vernon, waiting to be enlightened.

"What concerns me is that Samuel is only sixteen."

Chapter Five

Sixteen years old? Augusta hoped she did not look as astonished, as shocked, as she felt.

"Only *just* sixteen, I might add, this last April," the Baroness amended. "I realize that he might appear to be a man of twenty years, but the fact remains, he is not. And I cannot help but think that he may be a bit young to marry. There are fortune hunters and women who would take advantage of his situation." Lady Vernon glanced at Augusta. "Well, of course not you."

Sir Samuel was roughly the same age as her younger brother, Fredrick, who still attended Eton. She could not possibly marry someone that young. Could she?

"Do not allow Samuel's lecture about family and duty to influence you. I'm pleased that he finds those qualities admirable, but I am concerned, nonetheless, that he needs a bit of Town bronze that only attending a few Seasons will give him." She gazed kindly upon Augusta and continued. "I must compliment his taste and agree wholeheartedly of his choice. You are the first lady in which he has shown serious interest."

"You are most kind, Lady Vernon." Even though Sir Samuel was much younger than Augusta had thought, she could not eliminate him on his age alone. "I thought I might find a husband who is intelligent and thoughtful—age and appearance are merely superficialities. Both will alter in time."

"Goodness!" Lady Vernon brought her hand to her throat. "You are far wiser than your years. When one is young it tends to be difficult to see what lies under the charm and attractive façade of a young gentleman."

"I must confess that even I am carried away when there is music and dancing. I tend to forget what I am doing in London and cannot help but enjoy myself."

"And why should you not?" The Baroness giggled at Augusta's admission. "I have heard talk of a rush to throw last minute parties because of your late arrival. Even rumors of certain gentlemen who plan to return to Town solely to make your acquaintance."

How had Augusta missed this bit of news?

"One might speculate that arriving at the end of the Season would be a detriment. It has, however, not worked out as such. Can you tell me if this was intentional, and who, may I ask, contrived such a plan?"

"My father and my aunt, Mrs. Parker."

"Mrs. Parker . . . ah, yes. I believe she was widowed at a very young age, was she not? I seem to remember meeting her before she married many years ago, when she was known as Miss Penelope Darling." Lady Vernon sat in quiet contemplation for a moment. "I have not had the honor of meeting His Grace."

"I wonder if there should be an occasion where I could introduce the two of you?"

"I cannot imagine so. I lead a very quiet life and very rarely socialize outside my house even though I am curious and so enjoy hearing of the world beyond these walls." She glanced toward her lush foliage lining the walls and spilling from pots everywhere. "What else do I need except the pleasure that my garden gives me?"

That was a shame. Lady Vernon did not appear to be older than her aunt Penny—unless not looking one's age ran in her family. In that case the Baroness might be anywhere between nineteen and forty.

"Feel free to call upon me again, if you might spare the time. I have enjoyed your company so much."

"Yes, I believe I shall. Thank you." Augusta held an unexpected fondness for Lady Vernon.

"And you will tell me how you are going along . . . and how many more men have fallen in love with you." Lady Vernon set her teacup on the table.

"I cannot imagine a more pleasant place, or a more amiable person to pass time with." Augusta had the distinct feeling she was not the only one who valued their budding friendship.

"Where are you off to tonight?"

"We will attend the theatre." Augusta did not wish to confess she had never been before. "However, I am not sure which."

"And tomorrow afternoon?" Lady Vernon's eyebrows rose in an all-knowing fashion. "I expect that there have been many a young gentleman to occupy your time."

Augusta's gaze dropped to her lap. "I am to visit Kew Gardens."

"Oh—the flora!" the Baroness exclaimed. "I am sure it will be an excellent outing."

"I expect you should like to visit there very much. Would Sir Samuel not accompany you?"

"He would be happy to do so if I should wish it, but I think not. I am quite content to remain here."

Augusta realized that, with the exception of sheer size, Kew Gardens may not have much to offer Lady Vernon. She had quite an impressive garden herself.

"You must return and tell me your impressions of the gardens—and of the theatre. And of all your new gentlemen acquaintances . . ."

"Yes, ma'am. I shall." Just listing the men she would see and the parties she'd be attending in the next few days made Augusta a bit dizzy. For there would surely be several new ones to add to her list.

Truth be told, Augusta was no closer to coming to a decision as to who might interest her. Every day that passed, the number of her male acquaintances grew but there was less time to truly know them.

Augusta was not entirely sure how she would decide.

"I have not seen you since Friday afternoon, Gusta!" Emily complained when Augusta, her father, and Mrs. Parker arrived to the Wilbankses' townhouse for the musical soiree Sunday evening.

"Did you go to the theatre last night?" Emily squeezed in before the arrival of the other guests could interrupt them. "And to Kew Gardens with Sir Benjamin this afternoon?"

"Yes, and yes, and—" Augusta smiled and curtsied at the Lord and Lady Weybourne, greeting them with, "It is so good to see you again, your lordship, your lady-ship."

"The theatre?" Emily reminded Augusta where their conversation had been interrupted.

"Oh, yes. It was delightful—I enjoyed myself enor-mously."

Emily pointed to a gentleman from behind her open fan. "I see the Weybournes have brought their spare, Mr. Chester Atwater, with them. Did you meet anyone of interest there?" Emily paused, seemingly rethinking her question. "I mean anyone *new*. Surely there was a line outside your box at intermission."

"Only the brave gentlemen dare approach." Augusta recalled the quiet interval. "It seems my father is a bit of a gargoyle. All of them were frightened away."

"He *is* a duke, and they cannot know him as we do—agreeable and kind-hearted."

"*We* know him to be that way, I doubt any of the vis-itors that night would agree with you." Augusta touched Emily's arm, attracting her attention. "We'll talk about this later. We need to concentrate on this evening."

"I expect you're right. I suppose I am nervous because I am to play the pianoforte tonight." Emily glanced around at the growing number of guests. "We'll have more than a goodly number of gentlemen in attendance. Look there"—she indicated as best she could without pointing—"It's Sir Thomas Granville and his friend Lord Tremaine. They are both very desirous to meet you, Gusta."

Augusta felt her face warm. She would have wished for some dancing to occupy her time instead of attempt-ing to converse with new gentlemen acquaintances.

After supper, Lord Arthur Masters escorted Augusta from the table to the large parlor, where the musical entertainment was to take place.

"Will you be entertaining us this evening?" Lord Arthur inquired, leading Augusta to a seat and occupying the one next to her.

To her great relief, she had already been informed that she was not to play. "How do you know that I even possess any sort of musical abilities?" She noticed that he had chosen their seats to one side of the room where they might not be surrounded by other guests.

"It would shock me to discover that you do not have even the most basic skill of the pianoforte." He lifted her arm and splayed her gloved fingers, admiring them. "How could you not play with this finger span?" He smoothed two fingers past her wrist and they came to rest on her forearm. "I would not be surprised if you played a string instrument as well."

Augusta could not imagine how he knew, but some considered her study of the violin scandalous.

"There is muscular definition in your forearm and much strength in your left arm." With firm pressure he pressed various spots, proving to himself that he had, indeed, been correct. "I am a student of the arts: music, sculpture, painting. The human form has a great appeal for me—" He cleared his throat. "Artistically speaking, that is."

"Of course." How else would Augusta interpret his meaning?

"Have you been to the British Museum?"

"I'm afraid I have not had the opportunity." She did

not inform him that exhibits and museums were mainly of interest to her youngest sister, Muriel.

"Then I offer myself as your guide. If you would allow me to accompany you one afternoon."

And she would. Augusta was not as curious to see the antiquities as she was in observing the behavior and demeanor of Lord Arthur Masters.

The following evening, Emily and Miriam giggled and passed in front of the boxes, dashed around the guests, milled about, and finally caught up with Augusta at Vauxhall Gardens.

"Where have you been?" Emily sounded anxious at the sight of her dear friend. It had been days since they'd met and had a chance to speak.

"You're nearly an hour late!" Miriam, sounding a bit peevish, scolded her cousin.

"I'm sorry. I've only returned home a few hours ago. I barely had time to change before leaving for Vauxhall." She had stepped out of her puce flounced walking dress immediately into her green-and-white striped cambric frock and donned the bonnet for which Lord Fieldstone had, so generously, supplied the ornamentation. She secretly hoped he might easily recognize her. Augusta glanced around for the last member of their foursome. "Where is Lizzie?"

"She has already left Town," Miriam supplied, apparently cross at Augusta for arriving late.

"We are also to leave in a few days." Emily was not pleased to miss whatever festivities remained.

"The Season is as good as finished already, and I am

to be married the day after tomorrow," Miriam interjected—as if Augusta did not know and was not constantly reminded of her cousin's good fortune in finding a husband at the very start of the Season.

Yes, yes, Augusta knew well enough. Miriam would soon be a married lady, married to an earl and becoming Countess Dawson. Augusta would call her Lady Dawson. The worst possible bit of this development had nothing to do with Miriam but with Augusta herself. She had no engagement in sight, not even a single prospect.

But what had she expected? Augusta had only been in Town for a week. She could not make such an important decision based upon a meeting or two. Perhaps some could but not she.

"Never fear, Em, only a few days remain," Augusta reassured her best friend. "I shall write you as you wrote to me earlier in the Season—and I shan't omit any details. Once I return to Faraday Hall we can once again look forward to our tête-à-têtes."

"Splendid, Gusta!" Emily's radiant smile returned to her face. How Augusta hated to see her friend suffer a fit of the dismals. "Now tell me why you are late. Where have you been?"

"The 'Change," Miriam announced in her know-it-all tone.

"Exeter Exchange! Was it as exciting as I've heard?" Emily wanted to know. "I've heard it is a terrifying place."

"It is not for the faint of heart, I can tell you that much." Augusta wondered where she should begin.

"Mr. Allendale," Miriam announced firmly. "Why don't you start there?"

"Oh, he is very wealthy *and* very handsome, don't you think, Mimi?" Augusta teased her cousin.

"He need not be so handsome if he is wealthy." Miriam's remark went by without a response from Emily or Augusta.

"I shall allow you to form your own opinion regarding Mr. Allendale," Augusta said to Emily. "As I said, visiting the Exeter Exchange can be unnerving."

Emily's eyes widened, obviously expecting to hear a frightful tale of Augusta's afternoon.

"From the street I heard sounds of . . ." Augusta paused, attempting to describe what she heard as accurately as she could. "Clearly some sort of animal sounds, and they were distinctly wild. Not any dog or cat, or even any type of farm animal I've known."

"Oh, dear." Emily cowered back and grabbed Miriam's arm.

"I must have displayed some fear, for Mr. Allendale not only drew my hand into the crook of his arm, he covered my hand with his own and asked me if I was sure I wished to proceed. He told me there were some young ladies who found viewing the menagerie quite frightening."

"And you continued on?" Emily gulped.

Augusta straightened. "I assured Mr. Allendale that I was made of sterner stuff than the typical young miss. However I found myself gripping the strings of my reticule very tightly and hoped it was indeed true."

"Oh, Augusta!" Miriam, who was not nearly as timid as Emily, began to show fear.

"With a devilish smile he chuckled and confessed that he had thought as much, and he motioned that we move forward. We entered the building and climbed up and up the stairs." Augusta paused, trying to recall her impressions, and perhaps a small part of her wished to tease Emily as well. "The noises grew louder and the pungent odor increased. I thought I might . . ." She paused again, bringing her fingertips to her lips at the vivid recollection. "We finally reached a landing where we were among several other couples who had paused, unable to catch their breath—a *clean* breath."

Miriam and Emily groaned and made unpleasant faces.

"We continued onward. Just as we walked into the first room . . ." Augusta nearly shivered as she recalled the incident. "There was a fearsome roar from a large cat, some sort of tiger. It was very ferocious and wild. It flattened its ears against its head, bared its long fangs. I leapt back—thank goodness Mr. Allendale was there to catch me."

"So what you're telling us is that you ended up in Mr. Allendale's arms," Miriam commented, putting an emphasis on her cousin's behavior that might have made it seem scandalous, instead of it being the result of the terror she'd experienced.

"I cannot deny it." Augusta smiled. Nearly all the unpleasant smells had receded when she'd snuggled up against him. She felt protected while wrapped in his strong arms. The scent of his sandalwood soap and the starch from his linen filled her every breath. She felt completely safe. "It could not be helped, really."

"That's enough of Mr. Allendale, if you please, Gusta." The wide smile that spread across Miriam's face must have been for the benefit of the approaching guests.

"These gentlemen are only interested in how close *they* can get to you."

Augusta leaned against the squabs of the carriage after the night's wonderful music and dancing. She had simply enjoyed the evening with her friends and many of the gentlemen known to her.

How would she fall asleep after all that excitement? She sat next to her aunt and across from her father in the carriage as they traveled home. As far as Augusta was concerned, the night was not long enough for her to dance her fill.

"Gusta," her father said without a smile and in a deep, very serious-sounding baritone, as if she had misbehaved.

"What is it, Papa?" She watched his shadow move on the window shade with the sway of the carriage, and she wondered if he was contemplating her deeds.

"Your aunt and I have been discussing your visit to Town."

Augusta glanced at Mrs. Parker, who wore the most stern expression, then back to her father. She could not imagine what she had done that they could complain about.

"Even though we delayed your arrival it seems you have accumulated a greater number of suitors than I ever could have anticipated."

And was Augusta to think she was at fault?

"What your father is saying is that you cannot possibly be expected to choose among them." Aunt Penny sounded sympathetic to Augusta's difficulty.

"We have decided to host a house party in a

fortnight's time. You shall decide which young ladies and gentlemen are to be invited."

This was delightful news. There best be plenty of music and dancing every evening if Augusta were to remain content.

"We shall, one by one, strike them from your list if you should decide they do not merit your affection."

"My beaux list—" Augusta whispered on a breath, and blinked in disbelief. Such a thing did exist for her and it was amazing she could put it to good use. She might need help compiling a list of ladies, and had no doubt that Emily could surely advise her.

"Yes, by all means, once you have given me the guest list, we shall prepare the invitations." Aunt Penny nodded, acknowledging what had to be done.

The Duke reached across the transport, holding his daughter's hand. "Do not concern yourself, my dear Gusta. The family will stand by your side as you sort through your suitors. We may even aid you in your decision. I am quite sure there is one fellow among them who you will find suitable as a husband."

Augusta smiled at her father and her aunt and then thought of her brother and sisters. She had nothing to fear. Her family was there. They would always be there to help, comfort, and support her.

Chapter Six

Augusta sent Emily a note early Tuesday morning. With her father's proposal of a house party, Augusta needed the aid of her dearest friend.

"A house party?" Emily blinked moments after arriving at Worth House. Augusta hadn't even allowed her the courtesy of removing her bonnet before relaying the news.

Granted the Wilbanks household would be topsy-turvy with their departure scheduled for early the following day, but Augusta simply could not do without her best friend's sage advice when it came to her guest list.

"Surely you cannot invite only gentlemen?" Emily removed her gloves and pelisse after climbing the stairs to Augusta's bedchamber.

All of Emily's outer garments lay upon the bed while they worked undisturbed, mulling over the various acquaintances they had made during Augusta's week in Town.

"It would look most peculiar, would it not?" Augusta agreed. Although her list of eligibles came easily to her, compiling a group of females was a more arduous task.

A pot of tea and bites of strawberry tarts gave them sustenance for the next hour, until a gift of sugar-coated orange rinds arrived from Sir Benjamin Pelfry, which greatly swayed Emily's opinion of the baronet.

If, by chance, any of the lovely ladies might take a fancy to any of the men, and if any of the gentlemen should prefer said young lady, Augusta would certainly give them her blessing.

She would never stand between a couple who wished to be together. As their plan for a house party turned out, it was not only a way to find a husband for Augusta. There were other young ladies who might benefit as well. Aunt Penny soon joined their discussion and a guest list was agreed upon to the satisfaction of all.

An unexpected invitation found Augusta and Mrs. Parker attending a dinner given by the Earl and Countess of Rushton the following evening. Augusta thought it curious how they came to be invited. It might have had something to do with the two other women who attended: Miss Constance Greenfield-Jones, accompanied by her mother, and Lord and Lady Sutherland's daughter, Miss Emma Sutherland. Both young ladies, as it happened, were also on the Faraday house party guest list.

The Earl and Countess of Rushton were welcoming and jolly, excellent hosts.

"A dozen!" Lady Rushton called out to one and all. "We have an even dozen at our table tonight."

"By gad! What a time we will have!" Lord Rushton chuckled and tugged at his gold-striped waistcoat.

At supper, Augusta had the good fortune to be seated across from the very attractive Viscount Marsdon and next to the equally dashing Lord William Felgate. It was impossible to say which gentleman was more handsome.

When the meal ended nearly two hours later, the ladies left the gentlemen to their port. The men did not remain in the dining room for long and joined the ladies in the front parlor.

Lord Marsdon entered first, asking Augusta to partner him in a game of whist with Lady Sutherland and Mrs. Greenfield-Jones. Lord Paul Bancroft swept in front of the hearth with Miss Sutherland on his arm, taking a turn about the room while Miss Greenfield-Jones sat upon the velvet sofa with Lord William, reading his palm and informing him of his fortuitous future.

After the card game had ended and a new game began, Lord Paul approached Augusta to remind her of their introduction by Lady Castlereagh at Almack's nearly a week ago. Although they had not shared a dance, he had sent violets the following day. He also made it clear he intended to hold her attention for as long as the current whist rubber lasted.

Apparently it was far too long as far as Lord William was concerned, so he told Augusta when it was his chance to speak to her privately.

"Since Lady Rushton was kind enough to arrange this party on my behalf, you would have thought I might have the benefit of your company, but it does not appear that has happened. This evening I discovered that Lord Marsdon and Lord Paul have the advantage of a previous acquaintance."

"You are mistaken, sir. I did not make the acquaintance of Lord Marsdon until this very evening," Augusta replied.

"As did I, and I must confess that I have taken an immediate dislike to the fellow." Lord William's obvious contrived disdain for the viscount made Augusta smile. "After playing several hands with Lord Marsdon and Twenty Questions with Lord Paul, I expect there is not much of your time to be had."

Augusta glanced at the two gentlemen who had been mentioned, now occupied with Miss Sutherland and Miss Greenfield-Jones, respectively. "I believe more than enough of the evening remains to partake in whatever you wish to occupy the few remaining moments left to us."

"I can tell you I do not wish to waste my time occupied with whist or loo, nor would I wish to partake in nonsensical chatter to discover some random animal, vegetable, or mineral you have set as an answer."

Augusta would admit that partaking in games might not be useful in deciding upon a spouse. It did, however, allow the participants to enjoy, or not, one another's company.

"I believe in her desperation to find guests, the countess resorted to near strangers. Dashed awkward to plan a party with only you, me, and your aunt in attendance. It would be an odd five attending instead of a satisfying even dozen, don't you think?"

It hadn't really mattered how many sat at the supper

table. What was more important were his intentions toward her.

"We best pretend to be occupied. Here—" He snatched up a tablet of paper and two pencils, motioning her to one side of the room. "Let us sketch each other—that way I might do as I truly wish—gaze upon you uncensured. Shall we step away from the others as not to be overheard?"

They moved to one side of the room, providing a bit of privacy for their conversation, and sat at a small table with good lighting. Augusta accepted a pencil and paper from him and set it on the table before her.

"I must make a confession, Lord William." Although she could appreciate a painting, a watercolor, or a drawing, Augusta had no aptitude for originating such art. "I cannot sketch."

"Nor can I—but let us keep that secret between us, shall we? We must do our best to mask our inadequacies. As a man in search of a wife, I am finding that a role in which I am often cast is that of a gentleman without faults." He settled back into the chair and set to work, his pencil moving over his paper.

Augusta spoke first. "Lady Rushton tells me you have just returned to Town."

"I hate to admit that after I arrived in the country I heard of a lady so lovely who had appeared after I had left." The smile from his lips spread to his eyes.

"You're supposed to be drawing," she whispered, interrupting his longing gaze.

"Ah, yes." He cleared his throat. "I was merely studying my subject at length."

Lord William was a clever one. Sketching one another, at least merely the pretense of doing so, gave them the opportunity to gaze a bit longer than what might be considered proper.

Augusta had thought him dashing after her first stolen glance at the supper table, but now that she had the occasion to truly behold his features, she thought him almost beautiful. He had wavy golden-blond hair, a fine, straight nose, and piercing light blue eyes. His firm wide jaw gave his face a masculine structure.

After a few strokes of his pencil he continued. "Where was I? Oh, yes, my London departure." His gaze focused on the paper before him. "I heard this lady caused such fervor that I had to see the creature for myself." Lord William met her stare and held her attention. "I must say, she has far more than mere beauty."

Augusta glanced down at her own work, feeling quite self-conscious. Would she ever grow accustomed to any man calling her beautiful? "And who told you of this Banbury story?"

"I can honestly say there has been no exaggeration."

She chuckled and prevented his frankness from causing her to laugh aloud.

"So you've returned to Town in search of a wife, have you?" She took his lead and jumped right to the heart of the matter, pretending the lady he spoke of was not her.

"I must commend you on your directness." Lord William glanced at her and smiled. If he was shocked he did not show it. "I must confess that I have never willingly stood in the petticoat line. However, last year a friend of mine wed an exceptional woman. My only regret is that I did not have the good fortune of meeting her first. My second is that I do not believe I would have had the good judgment to marry her."

"Are you in love with her, then?"

"No, I admire her, esteem her greatly." He glanced away as if considering his answer. "Sir Randall and Lady Trent are well suited. I do not desire to take his place, but it does put me in a mind to follow their example. Such an association could be of great benefit to me as well."

"An *association*?" What an unromantic thought that was.

"It is not my meaning to—" He stopped and chuckled, seemingly at himself. "I'm only saying that *if* such a lady exists for me, I should like to find her."

Well, that *sounded lovely.*

"I should be very happy if you were the lady." His pencil had slowed to a stop and his attention focused directly upon her. He stared deeply into her eyes.

Augusta felt something. It was a heartfelt, serious, very adult emotion she could not name. "I am flattered, Lord William." Her face warmed, and knowing she was blushing made her feel even more embarrassed. "And how would we know if we are capable of forming this *association* of which you speak?"

"Ah . . . ," he crooned knowingly. "It is not always immediately apparent. I believe such things require a bit of time. The glow of infatuation can be quite deceptive, and when one is considered somewhat prized, as something to be won . . ."

Is that what he thought? Could that be what any of her gentlemen suitors thought? A trophy to be awarded? Augusta had thought she would be the one to choose among the men.

"Well, gentlemen can become wrapped up in the competition itself and mistake it for the goal." He chuckled. "Let me just say that I believe when it comes to a man and a woman, I feel it best that nature take its course. There is more to a match than dowries, land settlements, and family agreements. It's two people who, I feel, should be of like mind, don't you think?"

"I thank you for your opinion, sir. You bring up aspects I had not considered." Augusta laid her pencil on the table, finished with her work. "Are you ready to reveal your masterpiece?"

With a lackluster sigh, Lord William glanced up from his work. "I certainly hope my lack of artistic talent does not reflect upon me unfavorably." He appeared honest, his words well thought out, and he had a certain charm about him Augusta found engaging.

"I have another confession to make." She blinked down at her drawing. "I did not sketch you. I could not bring myself to do so, lest you form a poor opinion of me."

As she could not draw human features, she drew hearts, a chain of hearts in one enormous heart shape in the middle of the paper.

"All right, no more excuses. We trade on the count of three." He held out his paper face down; Augusta mimicked him and waited. "One . . . two . . . three."

Augusta pulled his paper toward her, face up, revealing his drawing. She gazed at his paper and laughed with delight. He'd sketched overlapping hearts in the shape of one single large heart located in the center of the page.

They laughed at the uncanny coincidence. Lord

William spoke, "I honestly cannot say if we could make a successful match, but there is something to be said when two people's thoughts occupy the same page."

Penny, who sat next to the hearth with Lady Rushton, watched the scene between her niece and Lord William unfold.

"Oh, yes, they do seem to be rubbing together very well. I think there might be a match in the making, there. I could not be more pleased. He truly is a good boy, you know, Mrs. Parker," Lady Rushton whispered to Penny. "The one odd bit about him is he doesn't care for tea, but one gets used to it."

"I am quite delighted that you have come to see me again." Lady Vernon motioned to Augusta to sit at the veranda table.

"I fear this will be our last visit." Augusta had stopped by to see the Baroness two other times without Sir Samuel's escort. The last had been just after her visit to Kew Gardens with Sir Benjamin Pelfry.

"Oh, I am sorry to hear that. I have so looked forward to seeing you." The Baroness splashed a bit of milk in their cups, then poured tea.

"I shall miss coming by for a bit of sanity." Augusta stared into the garden, expecting she would never know the gardening secrets or whatever magic spell Lady Vernon cast over her plants that made them grow with such vigor.

Lady Vernon chuckled. "You have your suitors driving you half mad and your friends leading you by the hand the remainder of the way."

Augusta could not have phrased it any better herself.

"When are you to depart?" A notable sadness laced the Baroness's words.

"Miriam's wedding is tomorrow morning. My family will leave for Faraday Hall after the wedding breakfast." Augusta continued on, spouting her news. "Emily's parents, the Squire and Mrs. Wilbanks, her brother Richard, along with Miss Olivia Skeffington and her mother, left for Yewhill Grange yesterday. Richard and his fiancée will have their banns read this Sunday, and in two weeks' time they shall marry."

"I can see that saddens you."

"No, not really," Augusta did not quite lie, but it was not exactly the entire truth. "I am very happy for both couples."

Lady Vernon stared down into her teacup, and Augusta had the distinct feeling it was to avoid meeting her gaze. "I cannot help but think you might wish you were in a similar position."

Augusta set her teacup on the table and clasped her hands. "I would wish it for myself if I had made a successful match."

"Is there no hope?" Lady Vernon looked into Augusta's face—what had she expected to see? Perhaps the truth. "Do you think it too late now that the Season is over?"

"Oh! I forgot to tell you the best news." Augusta leaned forward with excitement. "We are to have a house party within a fortnight. Papa and Aunt Penny are making the arrangements."

"A house party so you should become better acquainted with *certain* gentlemen," Lady Vernon mused.

"What a wonderful idea, but the sheer number of males who must be involved—"

"I should not like to think all the men are there for my sole amusement. We did invite many ladies as well," Augusta replied. "And Sir Samuel has not been overlooked."

"How kind of you to have invited my nephew."

"I would not eliminate Sir Samuel because he has not reached his majority. There will also be gentlemen who have not seen theirs for some time." Augusta did not wish to refer to them as *old,* but she meant those who were quite a bit older than herself. "A difference of a few years, in either direction of mine, should not be a deciding factor. Although I should not wish to marry someone who is thirty years of age."

"You are very wise, my dear." Lady Vernon chuckled and touched Augusta's arm reassuringly.

"May I write to you?" Augusta waited, hoping the Baroness would not think her forward. After all, their acquaintance had not been long.

"I'd be delighted. I must know what happens—the intrigue, the gentlemen." Her eyes grew large with every phrase, and her smile brightened at the very thought.

"I hardly think there will be much intrigue, Lady Vernon."

"One never knows about these things," the Baroness remarked. "Especially when it comes to your sisters. From what you have told me, Charlotte could not be more of a friend to you. The younger one, Muriel, she sounds very precocious."

"They would never jeopardize my future." She hoped

not, anyway. "My father wouldn't hear of it. This is too important." Especially to Augusta.

"All those guests, all those gentlemen . . ." Lady Vernon shook her head as if not quite convinced. "There's no telling what your sisters will have in store. In any case, I'm sure I'll find your escapades well worth reading."

Chapter Seven

Two weeks later—Faraday Hall, Essex

They're in here, Your Grace." Aunt Penny pulled the heavy, multi-paneled door of the *Specula Alta* open wide. A precocious Muriel, age six, had named this "watchtower" with the bit of Latin she'd picked up from her brother's tutor.

Charlotte looked up from the papers before her to view the intruders while Muriel remained ever-vigilant to the task at the window.

The Duke and Mrs. Parker entered the old nursery, which the sisters had always used as an excellent vantage point. As children, they had watched the comings and goings of their parents' visitors.

Today, Charlotte and Muriel observed the arriving gentlemen coming up the drive that ran along the side of the house, leading the guests to the front main entrance. The young ladies with their mamas and/or chaperones who arrived the day before had not been nearly as noteworthy.

"What do you two think you are doing?" The Duke

waved his daughters away. "Move from that window at once. You are bound to be seen."

"Oh, Papa, none of them can see us all the way up here," Muriel, with her logic and uncommon sensibilities, replied. "We are much too sheltered in the corner, obscured by the decorative architectural embellishments and overabundance of ivy, to be noticed."

Charlotte and Muriel pressed their opera glasses to their eyes, inched forward, and once again peered out the large diamond-shaped glass panes.

"Nevertheless, you shall ruin our plans if you are seen before tomorrow evening, Charlotte," Mrs. Parker reminded her niece.

"Moo is the one insisting we catalog every gentleman's arrival."

The Duke chuckled, as had Charlotte when she first heard of her younger sister's tally.

"It's not exactly accurate, you understand." Muriel swept a handful of papers from the table to show their father and aunt.

"How can you possibly know *who* they are?" Mrs. Parker inquired.

"Char-Char is reading the letters from Gusta, Em, and Cousin Mimi, and we match the gentlemen as they arrive to their descriptions."

"I think we're doing quite well, actually," Charlotte admitted. They'd been stationed at the window for a good three hours, starting right after they'd breakfasted while the rest of the house slept.

"See there is Lord Fieldstone with the black barouche. The golden-haired gentleman in the forest green jacket is Sir Carlton Wingate." Muriel pointed out. "And that gentleman in the green phaeton who's nearly tall enough to peer in at us is Sir Warren Cantrell."

"They seem to have the right of it, Your Grace." Aunt Penny chuckled. "There is no fooling your daughters."

"How right you are, Mrs. Parker." The Duke of Faraday gathered his daughters in his arms and gave a hearty laugh. "There is nothing that cannot be accomplished when our family works toward a single purpose."

On the ground floor, Emily, Richard, and his fiancée, Miss Skeffington, strolled down the main corridor of Faraday Hall with Augusta.

"I understand you had an assortment of ladies arrive yesterday." Miss Skeffington looked around. "Where are they hiding themselves?"

"They're still abed, I'm afraid. Must be keeping Town hours." The men, the gentlemen—her suitors—were to arrive today. Augusta could not restrain the continual, heart-pounding lightness and anxiousness that resided within her.

"I see the orange trees have been brought out for display." Emily indicated the two specimens that each bore a half dozen fruit flanking the tall, arching window in the Grand Foyer.

Aunt Penny's footfalls sounded from the staircase. In evidence of her haste, the lace cap atop her head fluttered during her swift descent.

"Augusta, dear! You must stay clear of the public areas until after the gentlemen have arrived," Mrs. Parker warned, waving the small group away. "If you are spotted, there should be a to-do that—well, I should not wish to think on it. Please, Richard, see the ladies to the Citrus Parlor."

"By all means, Mrs. Parker. Ladies, this way, if you please." Richard led their group in a leisurely about-face, toward the small parlor in the rear of the house.

"Exactly how many gentlemen are invited, Lady Augusta?" Miss Skeffington asked.

"A dozen, I believe." Augusta turned to face the front door of Faraday Hall. Just beyond those doors the gentlemen visitors gathered and, perhaps among them, Augusta's future husband.

"His Grace and I added Lord Marsdon and Lord William Felgate when you made their acquaintance at the Rushtons' dinner party a few evenings before we returned home," Mrs. Parker amended. "That makes fourteen. As you will recall, Augusta, they returned to London with the express purpose of seeing you. We thought them most impressive and equally deserving of your notice."

"Goodness me, fourteen!" Miss Skeffington exclaimed.

"There were not as many young ladies who received invitations, you understand. I also expect they do not know the gentlemen were scheduled to arrive today, else the female guests would have awoken early and breakfasted in time to welcome the newcomers."

"I can just imagine the chaos that will ensue with only a few women being pursued by these many men—it's best I keep Miss Skeffington close." Richard placed his fiancée's delicate hand in the crook of his arm and laid his strong, protective hand over hers.

Theirs was not a love match, Augusta understood, and she pushed aside her slight discomfort at observing them together. It was a constant reminder of what she dearly wished—to find a husband. It appeared they were well-suited and enjoyed each other's company. Augusta hoped she would find an equally suitable arrangement. It was her most fervent wish that she would achieve a more affectionate attachment, but she somehow felt that would be extremely selfish and highly improbable.

"You need not worry, Mr. Wilbanks," Mrs. Parker assured him. "I would not be surprised to find only half their number remains by tomorrow."

Charlotte stood next to Muriel, gazing out the window from the *Specula Alta.* She had never seen so many men in one place before. She and Muriel watched them arrive, mingle, and finally enter the house. All those gentlemen . . . what were they about?

Where eligible young ladies, mamas, chaperones, and maids had swarmed Faraday Hall only the day before, the influx of gentlemen would continue throughout this day. Most of them traveled with their valets, who saw to the unloading of the luggage. Many of them presently congregated near the swan fountain on the other side of the main drive of Faraday Hall.

Giggling and laughter began to fill the upper floor corridors just before noon. Charlotte imagined the female guests had finally realized the house party would soon begin. Faraday Hall was a very busy household indeed.

The thought of sharing her home with these dozen or so masculine, attractive newcomers caused Charlotte's heart to race.

"What's wrong, Char-Char?" Muriel narrowed her eyes at her sister. "You've gone pale."

"There are so many of them." She felt her face warm, then she dropped her shawl from her shoulders, hoping it would cool her. "I am to attend the ball this evening. I do not know how I am to—"

"I cannot tell you how happy I am that my presence is *not* required." Muriel held the opera glasses firmly to her eyes.

"But you have studied with the dance master." All three sisters had spent months in lessons before Augusta's departure. "Why would you choose not to try your hand at—"

"I have no intention of dancing this or any other evening, Char-Char," Muriel declared with firm resolve.

"Oh, that is a shame. After all that time practicing." Charlotte blinked, wondering if her younger sister felt shy because of her age and needed a bit of encouragement. "You are really quite graceful and have a lovely form, you know."

Muriel lowered the glasses to regard Charlotte. "Thank you for the compliment but I cannot see the point in the attempt. I do not enjoy the exercise. Besides, those gentlemen will only have eyes for you and Gusta, not me."

"I see." She understood that Muriel, only very recently thirteen, might not be of an age to attract any gentlemen of Augusta's age. But Charlotte, two years younger than her eldest sister, could she truly be of any interest to them? "Moo, do you think I can expect a dozen gentlemen to pay court to me when my time comes?"

"Oh, I shouldn't think so." Muriel raised the glasses to her eyes once more.

Charlotte felt a bit calmer at her younger but wiser sister's pronouncement. Being in the company of numerous men made her nervous. Muriel was very clever and could usually see the right of any matter.

"I'd expect double their number."

Charlotte grabbed onto the edge of the windowsill. The various letters she held slipped from her hand, sliding to the floor. She closed her eyes and drew in a deep breath.

Oh, goodness.

By that evening, the ballroom at Faraday Hall had been cleaned, polished, and lit to perfection. The Duke and Mrs. Parker had made sure to invite some local ladies, enough to make the disproportionate number of male to female guests not so obvious.

Augusta wore a pink spotted muslin with a wide satin sash, matching her pink dancing slippers and the small rosebuds in her hair. The outfit was thought up by her and her aunt during their travel home from London.

Never one to allow idle time to pass, Lord Fieldstone stepped forward moments after Augusta entered, and Sir Warren Cantrell, close on the Viscount's heels, was the second to claim a dance. Lord Carlton Wingate, coming in third, insisted she reserve the supper dance for him.

After her dance with Sir Benjamin Pelfry, Mr. Allendale, and Lord Tremaine, she noticed Lord William Felgate and local baronet Sir Nicholas Petersham in conversation with Miss Eleanor Jessop across the room.

Despite the men outnumbering the women, Augusta thought everyone behaved in a civilized manner.

During the final steps of the current dance, Augusta pulled her foot from under Lord Arthur Master's errant misstep. Her sharp glance at his face told her he was not attending. He had stopped dancing and merely stared toward the entrance.

"Who, I say, who is that . . . *creature*?"

Augusta could have guessed he wanted to use the adjective *lovely*, *becoming*, or simply *magnificent*, but her presence had prohibited him from showing outright interest.

Augusta glanced over her shoulder. "That, Lord Arthur, is my younger sister Lady Charlotte."

Charlotte entered the ballroom just after nine o'clock. Several wide pale blonde ringlets framed her face, and the golden threads which shot through the white silk of her gown shimmered under the crystal chandeliers above her.

At sixteen years of age, making a match was not even a consideration she entertained. Her father told her it was not her gown, or the metallic reflections sparkling from the material, but her own beauty that would blind the male guests.

Charlotte had attended many local assemblies and several balls. This gathering felt decidedly different. She herself could not prevent her insides from twisting or her hand from trembling, just a little. She was told how lovely she looked; she was told she would cause a stir among the gentlemen. Charlotte's presence, she was told, would aid Augusta in her search for a husband, and that made this uncomfortable endeavor worthwhile.

None of the guests knew of her true agenda.

Aunt Penny approached and made the introductions to the new guests she'd watched arrive that very day: handsome Mr. Allendale and elegant Lord Stanton. Charlotte didn't even mind having to share several dances with the likes of Sir Samuel Pruitt or the dashing Lord Marsdon.

Charlotte caught her bottom lip between her teeth, contemplating how stealing her sister's beaux might be unforgiveable but not unexpected.

"Are you enjoying yourself, Lady Charlotte?" Sir Thomas Granville uttered as they came together and moved apart in the steps of the dance.

"Immensely," Charlotte answered, then turned and stepped to one side and waited, the two of them being the "out" couple.

Sir Thomas gave Charlotte's hand a slight squeeze, drawing her attention from the dancers around them.

"I can no longer remain silent, Lady Charlotte. I must confess my great affection for you. I must see you away from these intrusive eyes . . . I must see you alone."

"Alone?" Charlotte did not need to feign surprise, his request had most certainly shocked her. "That is so very improper, sir."

"Yes, I know it is . . . but I—I cannot—" He broke off, as it was their time to rejoin their respective lines. In the final measures, the dancers made their bows, ending the dance.

Sir Thomas did not return Charlotte to the guests but pulled her to one side. "I *must* see you alone," he spoke urgently. "Please."

"I need a moment to—" Charlotte looked around to

see if they were attracting attention. "Walk me to the side door, if you please."

He acquiesced and they strolled to the opposite end of the room. Before reaching the guests milling about, she paused.

"Very well," she replied. "I shall meet you in the Music Room. Do you know where—"

"Yes, yes. I'll find it," he answered quickly, apparently rapturous over her decision.

"You must enter from the south door, through the Oriental Parlor."

"Yes, yes. I will." From his anxious, breathless reply, he sounded like a man who would agree to almost anything. "When? What time?"

"At midnight."

"But that is over two hours away!" he whispered in great anguish.

"I simply cannot leave the ball. It will look most peculiar to the other guests, to my family, to my father."

Sir Thomas Granville's posture noticeably stiffened at the reference to the Duke. "Very well, but I shall not know how I am to pass the minutes until I see you alone, my dearest."

"I imagine you will manage very well, sir," Charlotte said, wondering if he truly understood the entire deception.

They parted company, making their private exchange seem as normal as she could manage after making an appointment for a tryst.

"I've been watching you all evening." Richard had managed to catch Augusta between dances and Miss

Skeffington had the chance to introduce Augusta to her older brother.

Mr. Lawrence Skeffington was a tall pleasant gentleman with green eyes and wore his light brown hair *á la Brutus.* He was as handsome as Miss Skeffington was beautiful. Perhaps he would be fortunate enough to find his heart among the young ladies in attendance.

"You've still got your hands full," Richard commented. "Even though Char-Char is entertaining half your suitors."

"They are free to dance with whomever they wish. There is no reason they should follow in my shadow every moment." It could not have pleased Augusta more that the gentlemen could find ways of occupying themselves.

"Point well taken. You look lovely this evening." He stared as if truly admiring her.

"Thank you," Augusta replied with a somewhat cool demeanor. She thought perhaps he might follow his kind words with a teasing barb if he knew how much the compliment truly meant to her.

"You've been a veritable fashion plate in Town, but seeing you at home, in your own ballroom, where I have seen you numerous times before . . ." There was a catch in his voice that caused him to stop and clear his throat. "In any case, you are very lovely."

Augusta braved a glance at him now and graced him with a smile when she was certain of the sincerity of his words.

Richard glanced around. "Where is Lord Carlton? I heard he was quite insistent in claiming your supper dance."

"It appears even after his most sincere assurance that I have 'captured his heart' and he is so 'utterly, completely devoted to me,'" he has abandoned me." Augusta wasn't irritated by his absence as much as his persistence.

"Don't take it too hard, Gusta," Richard whispered, consoling her. "He was deeply in love with Miss Sutherland just before you arrived in Town, and to my dear Emily the week before that." He paused, seemingly thinking. "I cannot recall if it was Lady Julia Monroe or Miss Conway he had favored the week before that. No matter. It is known that he changes his mind—or should I say his heart—every few days. Faith, if he settled upon a young lady for a week's time . . . that would be momentous."

"And you are telling me this only now?" Augusta could not imagine why no one had mentioned his Lothario behavior.

"Sorry, hadn't thought of it."

Augusta let out an exasperated, unladylike huff. "Honestly, Richard, if I had known, I would not have invited him."

"Oh—you didn't think him exceptionally dashing, then?" He seemed truly shocked.

Augusta glared at her one-time friend with murderous intent.

"Only kidding," he said weakly. "Allow me to take his place for the supper dance."

"What of Miss Skeffington?" Augusta felt a twinge of vindictiveness at his jest and wished she could do him more harm than threaten him with a jealous fiancée.

"Oh, Livy is doing her part to distract your many

gentlemen guests." Richard chuckled, spotting her holding court, and did not seem the least bit concerned at his intended's all-male company. "There she is with Viscount Marsdon and Lord William Felgate."

"Fine." Augusta took Richard's arm and stepped toward the dance floor with him. If she could not successfully endanger his heart, perhaps treading on his toes with a misstep or two while dancing would do.

Chapter Eight

On exiting the supper room, Lord Perkins strode directly toward Charlotte and gently guided her to one side on her way to the ladies' room.

He, along with many of the gentlemen, had been glaring at Lord Carlton, who earlier had simply refused to be denied the pleasure of escorting her into supper.

While nibbling on the savories, Charlotte looked from one gentleman to the other, measuring their malicious glares and silent heated exchanges.

She marveled at the great discrepancy among them. Despite being light-haired or dark-haired, some were tall, some were not, and some of them exuded appeal, even across and down the length of the room. Some used their charm to flirt with her out in the open in front of everyone. As was Charlotte's disposition, she could not help but see the good in each and every one.

All of them in different ways were handsome and some of them were devilishly so. She could not look *at* them, for some of those gentlemen ignored the women next to them and stared with calf eyes at her for the following hour.

"I've a mind to seek out your father and offer for you tonight! What do you think about that, Lady Charlotte?" Lord Perkins, with his confident smile and overbearing attitude, threatened her.

"No—please," Charlotte beseeched. "My father will not sanction a match for me." An expression of utter devastation crossed Lord Perkins' face. She laid her gloved hand upon his sleeve. "It displeases me to see you so upset. I, too, think he might be a touch unreasonable."

Lord Perkins captured her hand and used it to draw her near. "Perhaps we could slip away," he whispered, lifting her hand to his lips. "Somewhere we could be alone, for some privacy to discuss the matter."

Charlotte turned her back to the room, preventing the majority of guests from witnessing the warm blush that washed over her cheeks.

"You are most persuasive, my lord." Charlotte smiled, and by his reaction she could quite believe that she had won him over—so easily. "*If* I were to agree to meet you . . ."

"Just name the place and the time—I shall be there." Lord Perkins gave her hand a small squeeze, and if Charlotte had not been mistaken, it was because he was anxious to hear the details she was about to lay out before him.

"The Music Room at midnight," she told him quickly, just above a whisper.

"But that is over an hour until—"

"You asked me to name the time and place and I have told you midnight." Charlotte had not meant to sound cross. If he did not agree to her terms, she simply would not meet him.

"I am sorry. It's just that I am most eager to—"

"Use the north door," she cut him off. "Its entrance is through the Citrus Parlor at the rear of the house. You'll find it unlocked."

"Twelve o'clock, then." He tightened his arm as if he meant to draw her near.

"Please leave me," Charlotte insisted, moving from him. "No one must suspect our plan."

"Very well." Lord Perkins relinquished her hand and reentered the supper room.

Charlotte moved in the direction of the guests, intending to return to the dance floor, only to find Sir Thomas Granville gazing longingly across the room at her. No doubt he was wondering if her ardor had cooled. Perhaps he grew concerned that she had forgotten their planned rendezvous.

No, Charlotte had not forgotten. She favored him with a smile and pulled her fan open with great care to cool herself and any passion she possessed, in hopes he would feel confident that her affection for him remained unchanged.

Her feelings for him had remained the same.

The handsome and very charming Lord Paul Bancroft approached her for the next set. Charlotte stepped onto the floor with him and the thought that he might ask something of her other than just a dance made it difficult for her to breathe.

While dancing, Lord Paul continued his overt flirting that he had started at supper. It had been quite a feat, since he sat near the opposite end of the room from her. But his smoldering eyes that made one feel as if a fire had ignited inside, and the touch of his gloved hand while sharing a dance, proved almost more than Charlotte could resist. And apparently, contact with her affected Lord Paul in a similar manner.

"You are the most beautiful woman I have ever seen," he murmured in her ear while close to her during the dance.

Charlotte glanced at Augusta and her partner Sir Samuel Pruitt, as they were the second couple in their foursome. Her elder sister did not seem to have heard Lord Paul's declaration.

"I am afraid I have forever lost my heart to you," Lord Paul uttered on the breath of a sigh before they parted for the final bow. "I must see you alone," he pleaded when the set had ended and he was leading her back to the edge of the dance floor.

"Alone? How can I—I suppose I could slip away . . ." She glanced at his dark, hungry eyes and replied, "If you could manage to—in ten minutes—find the Music Room. Go down this corridor and turn—"

Lord Paul nodded. "I know where it is." If he did not stop, it was entirely likely his head might fall from his shoulders.

"You must not be alarmed if you hear me stumble, for I am a bit clumsy and it will be dark, but rest assured I shall find you. Now we must part." Charlotte cast her gaze downward. She should not be making such arrangements. "We must step away from one another and no one should suspect that we have behaved in any type of inappropriate manner."

Oh, she did feel wicked.

"Richard, have you seen Char-Char?" Augusta had the good fortune to come upon him standing among the guests and she could secure his assistance in finding her wayward sibling.

"Were you not standing next to her in the last dance only moments ago?" Being taller, Richard could easily look above the crowd to spy the blond-haired Charlotte. "Where could she have gone?"

"I cannot imagine." How could Augusta have lost track of her sister so quickly?

"Richard, what *are* you doing?" Miss Skeffington joined in the conversation.

"I am trying to locate Lady Charlotte, pet." His head bobbed around, weaving to and fro as he continued his search.

"Oh. I see," Miss Skeffington remarked rather curtly.

By the obvious coolness of her tone, Augusta wondered what objection she could have regarding her sister.

"I do not see why *you* need locate her. I cannot like her, Richard," Miss Skeffington continued. "She is all that is false."

"What do you mean?" Augusta thought it was quite rude for Miss Skeffington to speak ill of her beloved Charlotte before her own family.

"I mean no disrespect, Lady Augusta. I will admit that she is a diamond of the first water—a diamond beyond compare, even." By Miss Skeffington's remorseless tone,

Augusta could tell she had no intention of apologizing. "I cannot believe that anyone possessing that amount of beauty could possibly be both thoughtful and accommodating. One normally finds ladies with those positive qualities quite . . . How shall I put it kindly? They are perhaps on the vain side and think well of themselves, very well, indeed."

Augusta felt her anger rise. How dare she speak about Charlotte in such a manner! Her fiancé may have close ties to the Worth sisters and speak freely about them at times, but that largess did not extend to Miss Skeffington—especially *before* her marriage.

"Oh, but I must disagree," Richard interceded before Augusta had a chance to vent. "Lady Charlotte is every bit the divine angel she appears. There is not a soul she does not think of before herself. She is everything that is generous and kind."

"Then where has she gone off to without notice?" Miss Skeffington replied in an effort to sound curious. "I hope she has not stolen one of your beaux."

Augusta displayed her superior deportment and manners by not responding.

"It seems she has quite disappeared." Miss Skeffington gestured, turning up her palms in surrender.

"She cannot have disappeared," Richard remarked and glanced at Augusta, who successfully restrained herself. "Charlotte must be *somewhere.*"

Charlotte waited in the Music Room. The time, one minute until midnight.

A soft rustle of fabric indicated someone moving about in the back of the room.

Charlotte had done precisely as her father had asked, following his instructions to the letter. Her heart beat in a tempo that would have been too rapid to play on the pianoforte or harp that sat at the front of the room.

A dull thump sounded from the right.

There was no *entrapment* involved. What Charlotte had done was simply given the gentlemen what they had asked for. However, the outcome might not be what they expected.

A scrape from a piece of furniture pierced the air before a strike flared, bringing much needed light to the Music Room. The single source of illumination wasn't enough to see anyone but the person seated, lighting the candle.

"Welcome to *my* gathering, gentlemen." The Duke of Faraday lit a second, then a third taper. Finally the last two, making five in all, revealed all the parties in attendance. "Please come closer, if you will."

Charlotte stood next to her aunt and together they flanked the Duke sitting at a small round table. The three gentlemen, Lord Perkins, Sir Thomas Granville, and Lord Paul Bancroft, reluctantly inched forward.

Lord Carlton, the fourth gentleman, was missing from their number. He had pressed her hand as he led her into supper, insisting they must meet alone, and she had instructed him to enter through the glass doors leading from the back garden.

"Unfortunately, for you this is a farewell party," His Grace informed them. "You three are each in the regrettable position of approaching my daughter Charlotte for what I would consider a most inappropriate *meeting*."

The gentlemen looked very uncomfortable, shifting

their weight from foot to foot, glancing about the room as if looking for a quick escape, and clearing their throats as if they could find their voices to refute the accusation.

"Without assassination to your characters, I shall merely say that the three of you have proven yourselves to be unsuitable, and I will ask you to leave Faraday Hall immediately."

With an expression of compliance, Lord Perkins replied, "If I may, Your Grace, I shall take my leave at first light."

"I mean *immediately*, my lord," Faraday insisted in a clear and forceful expression, a tone which Charlotte knew meant he was not to be disobeyed.

"But, Your Grace, it is the middle of the night," Sir Thomas protested.

"Let me be clear about this." The Duke stood, and Charlotte took a small step back, bracing herself, should her father choose to exhibit his anger. "I do not wish to see any of you at my breakfast table tomorrow morning."

"Ladies, Your Grace." Lord Paul dropped into an immediate bow and left. Sir Thomas and Lord Perkins followed his example and took their leave.

Their final leave.

Chapter Nine

Even after attending the ball until the early morning hours the night before, Charlotte was up and about before nine. She had breakfast in the privacy of her own room, and when she finally left, it was for the express purpose of seeking Muriel.

After checking Muriel's bedchamber and the *Specula Alta*, Charlotte thought for certain her sister would be in the *Librarium*. The small second-floor library was a place where, as children, they had spent many hours together, studying with their governess and Frederick's tutors before he reached the age when he could attend Eton.

As Charlotte understood it, Muriel could still be found in the *Librarium*, where she took comfort in being surrounded by her books. She usually sat in the far corner, where the sunlight poured in over her right shoulder, with her back against the rear bookcase that contained all her favorites.

Charlotte knew at once her search for Muriel had

come to an end upon entering the *Librarium* and seeing an open book held at head level.

"There were three of them last night, Moo," Charlotte reported. "Papa asked them to leave that very instant. He would not allow them to wait until daybreak."

The book lowered and a young, slender lad with straight hair, wearing spectacles, stared back at her. He stood, in fright, Charlotte guessed by the suddenness of his action, when he realized she had entered the room.

"Oh, I do beg your pardon." Charlotte felt very bad that she had disturbed him. "I thought you were my sister."

"Moo?" his voice cracked, as was common with a boy of his years.

"Her name is Muriel. Lady Muriel. Moo's a family nickname." Charlotte smiled. The young man must have been twelve or thirteen and stood no taller than her shoulder. "Who are you?"

"Sherwin Lloyd, my lady." He inclined his head just slightly, removed his glasses, and blinked back at her. "My brother James is here to—"

"Your brother is . . . Lord Marsdon, is he not?"

"Yes, that's right." He folded his spectacles and slipped them into his jacket pocket.

"I had the pleasure of making his acquaintance last night at the ball. I believe I danced with him. Were you also present?" Charlotte did not recall seeing him.

"No, I . . . I . . ." He tugged at his jacket, straightening the left side first, then the right.

He was far too shy even to admit he had not attended.

"You should have, you know."

"I couldn't possibly. I hope it is all right that I am here."

Young Mr. Lloyd sounded quite nervous and his prominent Adam's apple moved when he tried to swallow. "I was told that I could—"

"I beg you to please remain." Charlotte smiled, trying to put him at ease. "You are exactly where you should be."

"Here you are, Char-Char. Who is that you are talking to?" Muriel silenced when she saw the young man in *her* room with Charlotte.

Charlotte thought Muriel, upon spotting Mr. Lloyd in her domain, might have felt a bit territorial.

"Muriel, this is Lord Marsdon's younger brother, Mr. Sherwin Lloyd." Charlotte was happy to make the introduction. "Mr. Lloyd, my sister, Lady Muriel."

"Lady Muriel." He inclined his head, making her acquaintance. He shifted the book in his arms, adjusting his hold. His index finger held the place where he'd stopped reading.

"I have news for you," Charlotte whispered, then glanced to Mr. Lloyd. "I'll wait for you in your bedchamber." She looked from one to the other. "Perhaps you two should talk. It seems you have at least one thing in common—books." Then she left.

"Books!" Muriel groused. "She says it as if they were all the same. What are you reading there?" She indicated the book in his arms.

It so happened that Mr. Lloyd was reading *her* book. Muriel wanted to know exactly what subject he found interesting in *her* study.

"Ah . . ." He cleared his throat and turned the tome to see its cover. "The second volume of Publius Vergilius Maro's *Aeneid*."

"That edition is not translated. You *read* Latin?" She ventured carefully, feeling excitement bubble up inside her.

"Yes, and Greek. My main course of study at Eton is Classics." His voice sounded stronger now.

"You attend Eton?" How Muriel envied him. This young man was about her age, and if she'd had the freedom to attend Eton, they might have been classmates.

"I've just finished my first year."

"My brother is a third year. Fredrick, Earl of Brent."

"I'm afraid I don't know of him." He shook his head.

"I've been writing to Headmaster Keate. Here's his latest reply." Muriel tapped the sealed missive she held and raised her chin in defiance. "I'm petitioning to have female students admitted."

She knew the majority believed her request was futile, that the school should remain *all male* as it had for hundreds of years.

"No!" he said, more in astonishment than disapproval. "Have you had any luck swaying their opinion?"

"No, but I'm not about to give up. There is no reason why girls should not attend. They need formal education just as much as boys."

"I heartily agree," he replied with stern conviction.

It gratified Muriel to have someone, albeit one no more than a lad himself, not even as tall as she, share her opinion.

"I sat in on Freddie's Latin instruction when he was at home. I study the best I can now, but my father will not allow me the benefit of my own tutor." Muriel stiffened. "He does not wish to encourage me to follow what he considers male pursuits."

"I do not think acquisition of knowledge is foolish." He laid the book on the table and stepped forward to better address her.

"Thank you." Even the opinion of a stranger, a new acquaintance, caused Muriel to feel vindicated.

"Latin is quite fascinating." He somehow lost that air of awkwardness he had so firmly possessed when she first entered.

"I think so too." Muriel smiled at him. Young Mr. Lloyd was a fair companion . . . for a boy.

"To read *Aeneid* in its native text is a phenomenal feat. Some think Homer's *Odyssey* is a much better story. *Odyssey* is, of course, a longer journey, whereas *Aeneid* is only twelve volumes." He moved along the table, coming closer to her.

"But *Odyssey* is written in Greek. I can only dream of studying that language. As it is, I'm afraid I've only had minimal instruction in Latin. I find the Romans' way of life, their advancements, fascinating. Everything about them is so interesting." Muriel stepped into the room toward the window, toward him.

"I know of a tutor, he's in London." Mr. Lloyd pulled a stub of pencil and a bit of paper from his pocket and leaned toward the table to write. "If you are ever in Town, you should look him up."

Mr. Lloyd held out the slip of paper to Muriel. Another two steps brought her to the window that overlooked the parterre. She took the tutor's name and address he held out to her: Signor Biondi, 4 Tavistock Road. She realized that this was something quite precious.

"Thank you." Muriel could not meet his gaze and thought herself a goose.

He took in her tightly bound dark hair and conservative attire. Perhaps he was a bit intimidated by her, thinking she was much older than he. She glanced out the window, where a group of gentlemen guests congregated.

Mr. Lloyd followed her example. "Besides having cheroots, what do you suppose that is about?"

Muriel drew her opera glasses from her pocket and brought them to her eyes. The suitors, most but not all, were lounging about the marble benches blowing clouds.

"They appear quite amiable to one another even though they are in competition for Lady Augusta." Mr. Lloyd's voice seemed to constrict. "I don't think I could pretend friendliness, especially with *that* sort of company."

"What do you mean?" Muriel drew the glasses from her eyes to glare at him. "I'm sure you'd rub along with them quite well."

"No, I'm far too shy—especially when it comes to females—especially talking to females." He sounded nervous uttering the word.

"*I* am a female, Mr. Lloyd!" Muriel took exception to his doubt of her sex. She once again brought the glasses to her eyes and continued to study the men below.

"I beg your pardon, Lady M-Muriel," he stammered. "You are d-different fr-from other—"

"Please don't address me as *Lady*. It makes me sound so old."

His gaze darted away from her and he looked out the window, watching the gentlemen below. "I wonder what they could possibly be saying."

"Your brother is asking Sir Nicholas of *his* odds at

engaging my sister's interest," Muriel told Mr. Lloyd without thinking how inappropriate their topic might have been.

"Odds? As in wagering?"

"Exactly." Muriel concentrated on the precise reply. "Sir Nicholas gives him fifteen to one and tells your brother Lady Augusta thinks him no better than any of his contemporaries. He might have an advantage if he could show his superiority by besting the young lady in a battle of wits, because she does show a preference for verbal dueling."

Even without the benefit of magnification, Mr. Lloyd could see the reaction as the surrounding men laughed in good humor.

"Your brother says he'd not place a wager while on the Duke's property, because if they are discovered, they'll not have a chance to explain their actions before being expelled. Sir Warren is impressed with your brother and says he'll stake a quid on your brother's matrimonial future."

Lord Tremaine and Sir Warren Cantrell had moved forward, blocking Muriel's view of Lord Marsdon's reply. A roar of laughter followed.

"They're making bets on who wins Lady Augusta's hand? How can you know that's what they are saying?" Young Mr. Lloyd appeared affronted at the conversation and, it seemed, he refused to believe it.

"I observe them speaking, how they form the words with their mouths. I watch them and I know what they are saying."

"Is it possible?" Mr. Lloyd stared at Muriel. "Can you really do such a thing?"

"Not only can I do it, Mr. Lloyd, but I do it well. Why don't you join the gentlemen below and have a word with your brother and see if that is not what nefarious activity they have chosen to occupy their time."

Mr. Lloyd straightened and it seemed he was plucking up the nerve to do just as she suggested.

"My father will certainly give birth to a bovine if he should learn of this. Gusta isn't going to be pleased either." Muriel kept watch, studying the other men who gathered around for what appeared to be more betting.

"I don't see why she should be. It's appalling, reprehensible behavior."

Muriel pocketed her opera glasses, concluding her eavesdropping. "If you will excuse me, my sister Charlotte is waiting to speak to me." Muriel left, pleased that she had made the acquaintance of Mr. Sherwin Lloyd. She believed that, for once, this young man might appreciate her books as much as she did.

Chapter Ten

Augusta had risen to a wonderful morning and shared a fairly sedate breakfast with only seven gentlemen in attendance, exactly enough to fill every seat at the table without crowding. She did not know how she managed to successfully leave with one gentleman without making the other six feel left out.

Lord William Felgate escorted her down the corridor and into the foyer on their way to take a turn in the rear gardens. Perhaps she would show him the conservatory or the maze. Perhaps she would convince him they needed to drift along the water's edge of the pond.

Marriage to him, if Augusta were of a mind to select him, should be amenable. She considered that gazing upon his handsome visage for the remainder of her life would not be a hardship.

As far as Augusta had discerned, Lord William would seem an ideal choice of husband, with his lightheartedness, good humor, and joviality.

Then she, once again, reminded herself that he was not the only suitor in attendance, and it had only been a day since their arrival.

As they came upon the orange trees with their modest offerings of four fruit each, the massive front door of Faraday Hall swung open. A red and gold liveried footman stepped inside, allowing newly arrived guests admittance.

"Lady Augusta!" Richard's voice called from the entrance. He led his fiancée forward.

"Mr. Wilbanks," Augusta greeted them. "Miss Skeffington, good afternoon."

"Good day to you, Lady Augusta and to . . ." Miss Skeffington paused.

"Lord William Felgate, at your service." Lord William executed a splendid bow with Augusta dangling on his arm. "We were introduced last night, Miss Skeffington, but our meeting was brief."

"Is Moo . . . Muriel—Lady Muriel about?" Richard sounded a bit hurried and quite anxious to move along.

"I expect you can find her where you can always find her . . . in the—" Augusta supplied.

"The *Librarium*," Richard finished. He glanced at Miss Skeffington then back at Augusta.

"Is Emily here with you?" Augusta expected she was but had not seen her.

"She and Mr. Skeffington are occupied with Miss Randolph, Miss Sutherland, and some of the other gentlemen . . . off for some type of frolic, I expect." Richard took a step, then two, up the stairs, apparently anxious to leave. "If you don't mind, Livy, I just want to pop up for a few minutes to see Moo, er—Lady Muriel."

"As you wish." Miss Skeffington shrugged, withdrawing her hand from his arm to free him to take his leave.

"Perhaps Miss Skeffington will accompany us to the rear gardens?" Augusta could not very well leave Richard's fiancée to stand alone at the foot of the stairs.

"Sounds splendid. Why don't you join them?" Richard dashed up the stairs after giving his hasty approval.

Augusta caught Miss Skeffington's shy smile.

"I would be delighted." Miss Skeffington slid her hand through Lord William's proffered arm.

"Am I not the luckiest man? I have the pleasure of escorting not one, but two lovely ladies. One on each arm!" His already smiling face brightened even more so. "I am veritably surrounded by female loveliness!"

Augusta could not help but laugh, joining Miss Skeffington's high-pitched giggle at Lord William's pronouncement.

"Oh, Lord William, Mr. Wilbanks will be quite cross with you for saying such things," Miss Skeffington scolded.

"But it is true, is it not?" Lord William turned to Augusta for her opinion.

"I am sure he would completely concur." Augusta thought there could not be a more agreeable gentleman than Lord William.

"Right, then. Shall we be off?" Lord William led the ladies out of the foyer, down the corridor, and out the rear of the house.

The three walked leisurely through the rear garden and passed on the east side of the conservatory and orangery. Augusta pointed out the pond off to the south. They continued forward to the stables to visit the horses.

The barn—the first barn—held mostly the saddle mounts. There were the equines that had the most personal contact with the family.

The ladies moved away from Lord William to approach the individual stalls.

"Splendid confirmation," Lord William praised Damocles. "He has an intelligent look to him."

"My father's mount."

"And why shouldn't he have the best?" Lord William remarked. "Or two or three. Has he a hunter?"

"Plato. He's down three stalls."

Miss Skeffington followed behind Lord William a few paces to view the gelding.

"I say, he's a dandy, all right." Plato's soft nose settled into Lord William's hand. "And a jolly good disposition too."

Miss Skeffington, who apparently felt safe enough with Lord William's assessment of Plato, stepped closer and patted his neck.

Footfalls sounded, growing louder. Soon Richard appeared at the doorway.

"I beg your pardon. I hope I'm not disturbing you." He kept his distance from the group, and Augusta wondered, when was he ever not welcomed in her company?

"We're admiring His Grace's horses," Miss Skeffington told him.

"There is much to admire. Please take your time. I'd like to have a word with Augusta."

Augusta did not care for the sound of the declaration.

She moved to the next stall, across the aisle from where Miss Skeffington and Lord William stood. Richard strode to Augusta's side.

"Moo tells me three gentlemen were asked to leave last night," Richard said just above a whisper.

"I am aware of who was asked to leave, thank you. Papa informed me this morning." Augusta stroked Orion's arched neck, then proceeded to the next stall.

"I thought the news might be upsetting to you." Richard sounded concerned but he really needn't have been.

"Why on earth would you think it would upset me?" Who had appointed Richard her keeper?

"Well, they were lured by Charlotte. I am quite certain it was not of her doing—"

"As am I," Augusta agreed. "I should not be angry at Char-Char but those men . . . Good riddance, I say."

"Good riddance, indeed," Richard mimicked, albeit appearing relieved.

"As it happens, I am in debt to Char-Char for removing the undesirables."

"There are beaux aplenty, Gusta, do not lose heart." Richard's supportive nature was not needed this time, but she felt fortunate she could rely on her good friend to not let her spirits sink. "Not a Blade or Blood among them. Lord Arthur and Sir Warren Cantrell will certainly come up to scratch with your slightest encouragement."

"I am not sure I wish to go so far as to encourage them." Augusta considered the two of them the more questionable gentlemen.

"Lord Marsdon, Lord Tremaine, and Sir Samuel Pruitt all appear to be fine fellows."

"Yes, they are, Richard." Augusta remained calm and humored her good friend.

"Mr. Allendale, Lord Stanton, Sir Benjamin Pelfry, and Lord William, here," he whispered the last name as not to be overheard, "show much promise, don't you think? All have good qualities."

"Yes, Richard. They're all splendid."

"Oh, yes, and we should not overlook Lord Fieldstone."

No, Augusta could hardly forget him. Among the gentlemen present, he still somehow managed to remain in a class all to himself.

"The viscount is an unparalleled catch." Richard was not telling Augusta anything she hadn't already heard nor reminded herself.

"That is what I understand, and I am flattered by his attention." Was Augusta foolish not to accept him outright? As yet he had not offered for her, thus she could not accept a proposal which she had not received.

Miss Skeffington's and Lord William's burst of laughter echoed throughout the building.

"There really is no reason you should take a personal interest in these matters," Augusta whispered for Richard's ears alone.

"But I *am* concerned, Gusta. You are my . . ." He paused, stared at her, and swallowed. "Friend."

That is not what he had meant to say.

This whole business of finding a husband was sounding more and more as if it were a horse race—odds and betting notwithstanding. Augusta needed the council of her father, her aunt, perhaps even her sisters. There were still too many men present. What she needed was a way to reduce their number.

"Who might this be?" Miss Skeffington called out, sounding enchanted, on approaching the pony in the end stall.

"That is Buttercup," Richard supplied. "My father's gift to the Worth sisters some years ago."

"But he's much too small for any of you to ride now."

"He's not for riding, he pulls the girls' cart." Richard left Augusta's side to greet the brown and white pony.

Buttercup nickered at Richard's approach. She had always liked him, and Augusta suspected he was just as fond of her.

Glancing outside, Augusta spied the various rigs owned by the guests: a black Tilbury, two curricles, a landaulet, and a high-perched green phaeton. Sir Warren's, if Augusta was not mistaken.

She turned to her small, well-worn cart pony and smiled when a perfectly brilliant idea came to her.

"Yes, Buttercup . . ."

"A drive in the country! It's a splendid idea, Lady Augusta." Sir Warren's mood brightened. "I'll have my phaeton readied at once!"

"I've already sent word." Augusta, in hopes that Sir Warren would accept her invitation, had retrieved her bonnet, gloves, and parasol.

"I'll need my hat and coat." He snapped for a footman to relay the message to his man at once before setting off for the stables.

Augusta needed two quick steps to every one of Sir Warren's long strides to keep up with him. It seemed he was just as excited for their outing as she. They slowed nearing the corner of the stable yard, where their transport would be standing ready for them.

"I'll wager I can get my cattle moving at least up to—" Sir Warren stared at Buttercup harnessed to the small cart and stopped in his tracks. "Is this some kind of a joke?"

"It's my pony Buttercup!" Augusta announced with enthusiasm, tying the ribbons of her bonnet under her chin. "You've been such a *sport* to give me a drive nearly every afternoon while I was in Town, I thought I would return the favor."

Sir Warren had been struck speechless, and perhaps by the expression on his face, thoughtless.

"Have no worry, Sir Warren. Buttercup is plenty strong. She can reliably relay the both of us to the Wild Rose for a refreshing glass of lemonade."

"Lem-on-ade, you say?" Sir Warren replied weakly.

"He's taken all three of us girls many times, sometimes four of us. There is no need to worry." Augusta led Sir Warren by the arm toward her cart, climbed in, and patted the seat beside her. "You may sit right there."

He stepped into the cart and a footman approached with a coat, a hat, and gloves. The hat Sir Warren placed upon his head and he accepted the coat and gloves, laying them across his knee.

Augusta put up her parasol and handed it to Sir Warren. "Hold this for me, please."

The baronet could not have looked any more dismal. Satisfied that they were ready to depart, Augusta took up the ribbons and called out, "Come on, Buttercup, let's go!"

The pony stepped out of the stable yard, down the drive, and onto the road. It might have seemed the cart hit every pebble and hole in the road. Augusta was sure they could have walked faster than they traveled. She glanced over at Sir Warren, who, she was fairly certain, was completely miserable.

After a good half hour she told him, "The Rose is just around that bend." They hit a large rock that, by Sir Warren's reaction, must have loosened every tooth in his mouth. Another twenty minutes later she announced, "There it is!" Augusta pointed to the establishment that lay far off in the distance. It took another twenty minutes to arrive.

"Afternoon, milady," Fred, the stable boy, greeted her.

"Good day, Fred. Will you water and watch over Buttercup for me while we step inside for some lemonade?"

"'Appy to, milady. Just as always."

Augusta led the way into the front door of the Wild Rose, and a dejected Sir Warren trailed behind her. The poor man had only lemonade to look forward to instead of a bracing shot of spirits, which might have given him the strength to endure the drive home.

The innkeeper placed them in Augusta's usual parlor, and Sir Warren sat, not bothering to remove his gloves, coat, or hat.

"It's a simple place, but the staff is friendly and they serve very nice lemonade—and it's close by." Augusta smiled in pure delight, for Sir Warren looked miserable.

She pulled off her gloves, removed her bonnet, and unbuttoned her pelisse, intending to relax.

"Yes, I can see—" Sir Warren's head made a quick turn, and his eyes widened as if something had caught his attention. "Will you excuse me for a few minutes?"

Augusta nodded and set her gloves and bonnet next to her parasol on a small table. A few minutes went by, then a few more.

Five minutes after the lemonade and a plate of biscuits had been delivered, Augusta decided not to wait for him.

Fifteen minutes later she began to wonder where Sir Warren had gone.

At twenty-five minutes, after she had finished her glass of lemonade, she moved from the table and ventured out of the parlor.

Toward the back of the establishment, behind the two closed doors, Augusta spotted Sir Warren, well occupied with a handful of cards in his left hand, and in the background she heard a roar from a group of gentlemen after the distinct crack of dice.

With his hat off, it seemed as if he were planning to remain far longer than he'd planned to remain in Augusta's company. She gathered her things, settled her bill, and stepped into her awaiting cart.

"Walk on, Buttercup," she called to the pony, clucked her tongue, and smiled as they left for home.

Chapter Eleven

Bet a guinea, get a guinea!" Sir Nicholas Petersham stood before his bright yellow phaeton, calling out to the other gentlemen gathering around him.

Through her opera glasses from the window of the *Librarium*, Muriel watched the local baronet and the group of male guests gathering around him.

"We each set a Golden Boy on the dash. If you can reach them in seven seconds, you can have them both!"

"I'm game, old man!" called out Lord Stanton, who stood off to one side, but where Muriel could see his face clearly.

Both gentlemen climbed onto the rig and seated themselves. Sir Nicholas held up his golden coin, then set it on the custom-built tray before them with great flourish. Lord Stanton dug in his vest pocket and pulled out his guinea, placing it next to the first coin.

"Seven seconds!" Sir Nicholas warned Lord Stanton, waving his whip in the air. "Ready, steady—go!" He cracked the whip and yelled, urging his team onward.

"What's going on?" Young Mr. Lloyd stepped into the *Librarium* in time to see Lord Stanton thrown back onto the seat of the vehicle. He leaned forward, stretching out his arm but was held back a good ten seconds.

By the exchanged glances among the throng of waiting gentlemen, they found the feat difficult to believe—even though they had seen it with their own eyes.

"What are you two looking at?" Charlotte, who must have been passing by, entered the room. She gazed out the window, observing what held Muriel's and Mr. Lloyd's attention. "*Eavesdropping* again, are you, Moo?"

"There goes Lord Tremaine!" Muriel announced. Charlotte and Mr. Lloyd stared as the yellow phaeton shot away from the gathered gentlemen and, for a second time, streaked down the drive.

"They each set a guinea on the tray before them," Muriel explained. "If the passenger can reach them during the first seven seconds of the ride, they are allowed to keep them both."

"Seems simple enough." Mr. Lloyd shrugged.

"With Sir Nicholas involved, I suspect some duplicity," Charlotte replied.

"Exactly," Muriel concurred. "And I fully expect everyone loses." She looked to Mr. Lloyd. "Do you happen to have a guinea I could borrow? I'll be happy to return it to you in a few minutes."

Mr. Lloyd checked his pockets, finally pulled out a coin, and held it out to her.

"Thank you." She took the guinea and handed Charlotte her opera glasses. "Mind these while I'm away, will you?" Muriel stepped from the window and out of the room.

"What is she going to do?" Mr. Lloyd did not know Muriel well, and Charlotte imagined it might shock him to learn what she was capable of.

"I expect she's about to challenge Sir Nicholas."

"She can't do that—she'll lose for certain." Mr. Lloyd retrieved the opera glasses from Charlotte to better watch the commotion below.

"Do not be so sure, Mr. Lloyd. Moo is very clever."

Holding the glasses to his eyes, Mr. Lloyd did his best to narrate what he saw below. "There she is. She's speaking to Sir Nicholas . . . I don't know exactly what. The men seem to be taken aback by her presence. Now they are laughing."

"They're laughing at Moo?" Charlotte could not imagine her younger sister allowing that to happen.

"No, wait. I think they're laughing at Sir Nicholas." Mr. Lloyd shook his head, apparently uncertain. "I cannot discern which . . . I wish I knew what they were saying."

"Muriel has mastered *that* particular skill quite well."

"At the moment, I'm thinking I'd best spend some time learning it myself." Once again he focused on the events before them. "I don't think Sir Nicholas wants her to participate, and she does not appear to be giving up the idea very easily. It seems she is being quite stubborn."

If only her sister could limit herself to *merely* stubborn. Sir Nicholas could not know how persistent Muriel could prove. Did he even suspect she would eventually achieve her end?

"Ah, success! Look there." Charlotte pointed out

Muriel stepping into the rig—being *hoisted into* was a more apt description—and Sir Nicholas climbing in after her.

"I cannot believe this." The opera glasses remained fixed before Mr. Lloyd's eyes.

Cheering from the onlookers accompanied the customary laying down of coins. Even from the *Librarium*, Charlotte could hear the shouts up until the moment the phaeton sped away.

The cheering stopped. The gentlemen stood quiet.

"What's happened?" Mr. Lloyd searched the immediate area for signs of the outcome. "I can't tell."

"I know what's happened." Charlotte smiled with full confidence in her sister.

A few minutes later the yellow phaeton returned—without Muriel, and the men cheered again.

"Where has she gone?" Mr. Lloyd again searched the area below.

Muriel stepped into the room, reappearing behind them, all smiles, holding up a guinea.

"Thank you, Mr. Lloyd." She held out her left palm, returning his coin. Muriel held up a second guinea in her right hand. "Now I have one too!"

Augusta left Buttercup and the cart at the stables and came striding down the corridor of Faraday Hall with purpose.

"Huxley," she called out while untying the ribbons of her bonnet.

"My lady?" the butler replied, coming to her side for further instruction.

"When Sir Warren returns, whenever that may be, he is to leave at once."

"I will inform his valet to prepare for their departure." Huxley bowed and set off to deliver the message.

"Thank you." Standing there for a moment, Augusta stared at the two orange trees flanking the arched window. Each bore only three fruit. She hadn't remembered them looking so bare.

Glancing around, she could not imagine where everyone had gone. Charlotte, Muriel, Mrs. Parker, the ladies, the gentlemen guests . . . amusing themselves somewhere, no doubt. Determined to join them in whatever activities they had chosen to occupy their time, Augusta first headed abovestairs to change her clothes.

Not two minutes after her abigail Lydia finished touching up Augusta's hair, there was a hurried knock at the door and Charlotte and Muriel entered the bedchamber.

"Char-Char and I have decided, Gusta," Muriel stated straightaway.

"Decided what, pray tell?" Augusta regarded her profile in the glass and moved the curled tendrils away from her face.

"You cannot settle upon Fieldstone," Charlotte informed her.

"Even Char-Char believes he is deadly flat," Muriel added.

Augusta's severe gaze darted to the middle sister, who stood composed. "Char-Char, how could you say such a thing?"

"That is not what I meant . . . not precisely," she confessed. "I merely wondered about his ability to see the humor in any situation . . . especially amusing ones. Although he does not seem to find much of anything to laugh at—for I have not observed him to even smile." It did not seem as if Charlotte were jesting in the least. "He appears to be awfully serious, Gusta. Do you think Viscount Fieldstone is able to laugh?"

"He is dull beyond belief!" Muriel interjected with a loud groan. "That man does not find humor in any situation! And Char-Char is correct. I cannot say I have ever seen him share in any of the amusements with the other gentlemen, not once. He did not even smile when he learned of the dismissal of several competitors that first night."

This treatment of Viscount Fieldstone was beyond enough. "Of course he can smile." Augusta quickly came to his defense. She tried to recall a single occurrence when he had graced her with a smile. To tell the truth, she could not think of one.

If he did not or could not find joy in any circumstance, was that cause to believe he had a temper? Surely everyone was angered at one time or another.

If Augusta married him, would she discover she had wed a thunderous ogre when his morning toast was near burnt? Would he rage out of control if he came across a smudge on the toe of his Hessian boots? But most importantly, could he, would he, ever share a comfortable laugh with her?

Augusta left her sisters in her bedchamber and headed for the hedge maze behind the rear gardens, thinking of what they had observed regarding Lord Fieldstone. She paced around her mother's statue in the center of the maze, somehow finding strength in her maternal parent's marble presence.

"What ails you, Gusta?" Richard's voice startled her.

"What?" Augusta spun to face him.

"I'm not disturbing you, am I?" Why should he ask? She always welcomed his company.

"No, Richard." She flashed a nervous, quick grin to show he was welcome and motioned for him to approach. "My sisters came to me, asking if . . . They had questions about the merits of . . ." Augusta felt a bit embarrassed, and thought she was behaving silly when she hesitated to utter, "Lord Fieldstone."

"Ah, Viscount Fieldstone," Richard repeated thoughtfully. "He is an admirable choice."

And he always had been very much admired up until now.

Augusta had hoped Richard knew something of Lord Fieldstone. Some unsavory behavior that would make a match with him impossible.

"Do Char-Char and Moo find fault with him? How? His reputation is unmarred. He would make an excellent match. I cannot see how even your father could reject him." Richard glanced at her. "If you find him agreeable . . . He is one of the eight gentlemen remaining."

"Eight?" Last Augusta had heard, ten remained. "Who has left us?"

"Lord Tremaine and Lord Stanton. Caught wagering with Sir Nicholas Petersham, who, by the bye, has been asked to make himself scarce. Your father was quite upset."

"Wagering on what?" She hadn't exactly kept abreast

of the day's goings-on, but she was certain Muriel could provide an exact account. No doubt this was where Richard received his updates.

"Some of the gentlemen were discussing the odds of other gentlemen in attendance. Sir Nicholas merely covered the bets." No doubt, Richard must have heard this from Muriel.

"It serves them right." Augusta huffed and exhaled and— Well, this did not please her. "When will anyone learn there is nothing to be gained by wagering?"

"I should not say that to Moo. She won a guinea from Sir Nicholas just this morning," he mumbled, and it did not go by unnoticed.

"Well, then, I suppose Sir Nicholas deserves to be outwitted by a twelve-year-old."

"She's thirteen now. You've forgotten her birthday again," Richard gently reminded her. "Where were we?" Apparently, he was anxious to move their conversation away from Sir Nicholas, or his wagering, or Muriel's besting of Sir Nicholas. "Ah, I believe we were discussing Lord Fieldstone's difficulty. Your reservation must be greater than his suitability, I wager."

Augusta shot him a sharp look at his last words.

"Oh, sorry." Richard cleared his throat, perhaps even trying to hide a bit of laughter, realizing his faux pas. "What do Moo and Char-Char find objectionable?"

Augusta exhaled, dropped her arms to her sides, and closed her weary eyes. "He may be most agreeable and all that is good, but they insist I should not have him."

Richard remained quiet and allowed her a moment of contemplation. Augusta did not want to tell him what she and her sisters had discussed, but she wished to confide in someone.

"Lord Fieldstone does not seem to . . ." Embarrassment caused her to stop, but Augusta decided she must tell him if she were to hear his opinion. "Richard, I do not think I can spend my life with a man who cannot laugh or show the least amount of joy, for that matter."

"Is he that type of man?" Richard seemed to doubt it as much as she had. "Then I suggest you do what you must to make sure he is *not* that kind of man."

"I should attempt to *make* him smile?" What a very odd thing to do.

"Oh, Gusta, if you are so concerned he is without humor, make him laugh!" That made Richard give in to his own deep, hearty laughter, stemming from his belly. "I'll admit Lord Fieldstone may be on the serious side, but I'm sure he is quite capable of displaying some type of humor. Come now, everyone is."

Perhaps Richard was right. Augusta should make the effort. That in itself sounded very silly. And what if Muriel and Charlotte had the right of it and the Viscount was devoid of any sense of frivolity?

"One never can tell what another finds humorous," Richard managed after calming himself. He'd stopped laughing, but the lingering joy in his eyes was evident. "I have an idea. Why don't you tell him the story about the time we went fishing. You had just turned ten and told me that you were old enough to bait your own hook and from then on you would be doing it yourself."

"*That* was not funny." She stood in firm disagreement. "That was a horrible ordeal—not only for the worm but for me as well."

"It *was* funny to everyone *except* you." Richard laughed as he always had in recalling what Augusta believed was a very painful tale.

Richard's words gave Augusta much to consider during her toilette that evening for the supper and music that would follow, where she would perform.

Augusta thought the meal was pleasant and fairly uneventful. The guests chatted amicably with those seated next to them. She enjoyed conversation with Lord William and Lord Marsdon. When the meal ended, she led the women to the Oriental Parlor so the men could enjoy their port.

"I cannot think of a single gentleman who would possibly be interested in any other young woman but Lady Augusta," Lady Sutherland complained. "They are all hers to do with as she likes!"

"You could not be further from the truth, Lady Sutherland," Mrs. Greenfield-Jones replied. "I caught one or two of them studying my Stanza here." Her daughter, Miss Constance, blushed.

If only the gentlemen could see that becoming reaction, Augusta thought, Miss Constance would quite capture their hearts.

"Now, now, Lady Sutherland," Mrs. Wilbanks, neighbor and friend to Augusta's family, addressed the accusation. "Every young lady has an equal chance with any of the gentlemen guests. If, indeed, a match is forthcoming."

"But it seems so obvious that the only reason we have been invited is to add some propriety to Lady Augusta's situation. It could not be clearer that every gentleman attending is a beau of hers!" The countess would not be silenced.

"I beg your pardon, Lady Sutherland," Miss Skeffington interjected. "That is not precisely true."

"Well, it just so happens that you have a prior, standing engagement to Mr. Wilbanks. Do you think you could ever bring him up to scratch on your own?" Lady Sutherland glared at Miss Skeffington most severely. "I think not."

"Lady Sutherland, you are being quite rude," Aunt Penny interrupted. "I beg you, do not distress the young ladies during this time. If my niece, or nieces, have an advantage, it is through no fault of their own."

"Imagine thinking that having an *advantage* is a fault!" Emily chuckled.

"I must assure you that no one, with the exception of Miss Skeffington here, has a claim over any gentlemen," Mrs. Parker assured her.

The deep rumble of male voices silenced the women, who immediately returned to their best behavior. Within minutes the guests conversed freely.

Sir Benjamin and Mr. Allendale managed to have a word with Augusta, having not done so during supper, but she could not dismiss thoughts of Lord Fieldstone and the dilemma he posed. She glanced in his direction. He stood in conversation with Lord Sutherland and acknowledged her with a nod.

Next to those two gentlemen, the very young Sir Samuel, who conversed with Charlotte and Mrs. Parker, did not prove to have such difficulties. Her father, her aunt, and both sisters liked him very much.

"We have a short program planned for tonight," the

Duke finally announced. "I fully expect our other guests to honor us with a display of their talents in the evenings to come."

Murmurs circulated throughout the room of who might be talented at which instrument and which piece might be played for the evening.

"Shall we proceed?" The Duke offered his arm to Charlotte and led the procession down the corridor to the Music Room.

Lord Arthur Masters was first to offer to escort Augusta.

"You are to play for us tonight?" he asked. "What a delight! I have been looking forward to this since the end of the Season."

"I managed to avoid it in Town but cannot do so in my own home. It should be quite rude of me."

"Shall you favor us with a selection on the *violin*?"

"We shall see, my lord," she teased him. "We shall see."

They stepped into the Music Room. Candles lit the large ornate walls, illuminating the coffered ceiling and decorative friezes. Four rows of chairs, ten wide with an aisle down the center, faced forward where the piano and harp sat.

Upon spotting the harp, Lord Arthur's eyes went wide. "Is it possible that you play the harp and not the violin?"

Augusta caught his steady gaze moving from her gloved hands to her wrists and up her forearms. Did he wish to grasp her arms and reexamine the musculature in her extremities, as he had before, to discern which instrument she played?

"You must be patient, my lord." Augusta relinquished her hold on his arm and moved away, allowing him to find a comfortable seat to observe the performance.

The short, puffed sleeves of her gown would give her ease of movement whether playing the harp or the violin. Augusta drew off her long kid gloves, exposing her forearms as she prepared to take up her instrument.

The case of nerves she felt had nothing to do with her performing, for she had played the pianoforte for most of her life, starting at a very young age, as had her sisters. They all took up additional instruments when proficiency of the pianoforte had been mastered.

Emily and Charlotte moved past the guests, settling to their chairs, joining Augusta. Emily sat at the pianoforte. Charlotte took her seat by her harp. From the credenza, Augusta retrieved her violin and bow, turned forward, and glanced at Lord Arthur, who winked at her in an I-knew-it manner.

The soft tapping of Emily's slipper on the pedal indicated the tempo and they would begin playing on the silent count of three. The music began.

After the first two measures, Lord Carlton murmured, "She plays like an angel!"

If Penny had not been sitting next to Lord Carlton she might not have heard his words.

"Yes, Lady Augusta is quite accomplished," Mr. Skeffington, who sat to Lord Carlton's right, acknowledged.

"No . . . Lady Charlotte." Apparently the act of uttering her name made him emotional. Lord Carlton's subsequent gasps were followed by a whimper.

Penny leaned in his direction to ask, "Are you quite all right, sir?"

"I have never heard such heavenly music in all my life!" was his reply. A heart-wrenching sob ensued.

"Lord Carlton, please," Penny said. "Come now, you must control yourself."

Miss Jessop, who sat behind him, was good enough to hand him her handkerchief, laying it over his shoulder.

"Thank you," Penny whispered. Lord Carlton nodded, apparently unable to speak.

A rippling arpeggio flowed from Charlotte's fingertips, which caused the tone of Lord Carlton's uncontrollable bawling to climb with the ascending notes. The concert continued; the musicians remained focused on their piece.

Penny motioned to the footmen standing in the doorway to approach. Mr. Skeffington moved from his seat, allowing the footmen to escort Lord Carlton from the seated guests and out of the room.

Once he had left, Penny glanced about to ascertain how much of a disturbance he had created. Of course, everyone had heard him cry out, more than a few times, and could not but notice him bodily removed from the Music Room.

It was embarrassing and disgraceful, for Lord Carlton and the observers. Penny settled into her seat and focused forward, trying to put the incident behind her. She expected that once he managed to pull himself together, he would come to his senses and do what was expected: remove himself from Faraday Hall.

Chapter Twelve

The next morning after breakfast, Augusta had managed, without much difficulty, to persuade Lord Fieldstone to accompany her to the *Lapidarium*, a natural outcropping of stones, named by Muriel, that comprised a garden overlook that had been formalized when the Duke had a roof and steps added some years back.

While walking from the terrace to the *Lapidarium*, Augusta thought perhaps this might be her chance to sate her curiosity.

"I enjoyed your performance last night," he told her. "Some believe that it is quite risqué for a lady to play the violin."

"It is only an instrument, my lord. Drawing the bow over its strings would no more cause me to go to the devil than playing the harp would guarantee me entrance into Heaven."

"I believe Lord Carlton declared it probable last night."

Had that been a joke? Augusta stared at him. The Viscount was not laughing, nor had the corners of his mouth turned up in a smile.

He turned from her and took note of their surroundings. "I must commend your family on their upkeep of your home," Lord Fieldstone told her after she fastened the ribbons of her bonnet and slipped her hand into the crook of his arm. "Faraday Hall has splendid grounds, immaculately cared for."

"We have always enjoyed living here," Augusta replied. "As children we made good use of the maze in particular." She watched his responses carefully. "We also helped ourselves to the carrots out of the garden to feed to the horses, and we thought the kitchen staff would never miss them."

His eyes widened just a touch before he commented, "I would venture to say that you were wrong."

"Probably, but they never scolded us."

"Ah, you were *wild* children then," he jested, at least Augusta hoped it was such.

"Completely out of hand!" She chuckled, hoping he would follow her lead and do the same. "Here we are."

They came to a halt before the ivy-covered, small stone elevated structure off in one corner of the rear gardens, and most important, just outside the maze.

She lifted the hem of her skirt and preceded him up the five steps.

"My word, what a sight," Lord Fieldstone exclaimed, taking in the view. "This is amazing."

"Papa had this small pavilion built so we could see the center of the maze, just in case we were to lose our way."

She pointed at the tall hedges. "You see the animal topiary on the outside? They mark the different paths."

"I see a camel, a lion, an elephant, and a giraffe."

"That's right. I believe the real reason for constructing this lookout was so he could find us when we hid from him. We were *wild* children, if you will recall."

"Ah, yes. Your father is an astute man. There is no use fighting what he cannot control."

"Exactly." Augusta glanced at him from the corner of her eye to see if she'd managed to coax even the smallest smile from him.

She had not.

Sterner measures were called for. Augusta thought perhaps it best if she were to ask him outright. "Lord Fieldstone, do you ever have any *fun*?"

"Fun?" Lord Fieldstone gazed at Augusta, narrowing his eyes. "I have had my fair share of fun, I can assure you."

What concerned Augusta was that he did not deny it with a smile.

"I enjoy many pleasurable activities, from collecting snuff boxes to walking sticks, and drizzling on occasion."

That was a relief to hear. He did engage in enjoyable pursuits. Although tugging gold threads free from old tapestries was not how she imagined him passing his free hours. Augusta could not find it in her to become excited at the thought he might have some lovely spool boxes that rivaled his snuff box collection.

Still the Viscount did not smile, nor did he elaborate on his hobbies. What he did was abruptly change the subject. "What lies beyond the conservatory?"

"The orchard to the west, moving south there's the stables and then the pond." Augusta pointed to the manor's edge, far beyond the rear garden, opposite the maze. "One can see the water better from the knot garden."

Augusta was so desperate for him to smile that she finally told him the story of the first, and only, time she baited her fishhook. She regarded him after the tale and could not even decide if he enjoyed the anecdote.

"Ah, yes. That is quite charming, very amusing."

But this did not alter his staid expression.

"What a delightful child you were—filled with curiosity and very brave," he commented in a tone that conveyed his satisfaction.

He thought it was just as humorous as Augusta had.

Either he was incapable of smiling or Richard had been wrong. The story was not funny.

"Well?" Muriel and Charlotte sat in Augusta's bedchamber, waiting to hear the outcome of Lord Fieldstone's interview.

Augusta glanced at each of them in turn and walked by. Could they not wait until she changed her clothes? Until she sat? Even for two minutes?

"It appears the Viscount is incapable of laughter," Augusta told her sisters as she sat at her dressing table. "I cannot find the smallest evidence of joviality in him."

"I knew it, the man is as dull as dishwater." Muriel brightened in the knowledge that she had been correct.

"Oh, I am sorry, Gusta. Does that make you think less of him?" With a tilt of her head, Charlotte's sympathy threatened to overwhelm Augusta.

She did not want sympathy of any kind. There was no shame if Lord Fieldstone was not the man she thought him to be, the man she would have wished him to be.

"It is of no consequence. There are many other gentlemen and there must be at least one among them who you will find agreeable." Charlotte turned her face away and whispered something to herself or to Muriel, but clearly, it was not meant for Augusta's ears.

"What is that you're saying, Char-Char?" Augusta urged her sister with a pat on her arm, then glanced at Muriel, trying to decipher what new complication her sisters had planned for her.

"I'm afraid we really must insist, Gusta," Charlotte repeated a bit louder.

Augusta stared at Muriel, counting on the comprehensive explanation that would soon follow.

"Char-Char means Lord *Ce-treece*, Gusta," she enunciated quite distinctly.

"Who?" Augusta could not recall any gentleman by that name.

"Moo, do stop," Charlotte scolded. "We call him by that name so no one will know to whom we are referring."

"Unfortunately, you include me." Augusta stood, crossed her arms, and waited for clarification.

"Moo is speaking of—" Charlotte glanced about to make certain they were not overheard, and whispered, "Sir Benjamin Pelfry."

Augusta felt quite taken aback. "Sir Benjamin? He is perfectly agreeable and most amiable. I have even seen him laugh on more than one occasion."

"He is completely addle-brained, perhaps even mad,"

Muriel interrupted, quite passionate in her response. "I believe *deviant* would not be too harsh a term."

Both Charlotte and Augusta gasped.

"This very morning that man told me that I was to retreat from the small pitcher of orangeade on the sideboard in the breakfast room."

"Whatever for?" Odd behavior, perhaps, but Augusta could not conceive why that would make him a *deviant.*

Muriel affected an air, imitating the baronet, and continued, "I could not possibly *appreciate* the finer qualities of a freshly prepared citrus extract."

"He was speaking of a beverage, was he not?" Charlotte must have not been sure she had understood correctly.

"Yes," Muriel said with a firm nod. "I'm telling you, Gusta, that man has an unnatural affection for fruit, citrus in particular. I heard that he even asks for sliced lemon for his *tea.*"

Even Charlotte could not suppress a small cringe.

"I would not be shocked to discover that he had been pinching the oranges from the foyer trees!" Muriel's voice rose with the heated accusation. "The two trees standing in the Grand Foyer, have you noticed the number of fruit decreasing?"

Augusta had.

Citrus? There was something about citrus . . . and oranges in particular . . . Augusta tried to recall. A month ago while she was in Town, Sir Benjamin had sent a tribute of sweet-smelling orange blossoms tied with a white satin ribbon. The day after their visit to Kew Gardens he had sent her candied orange rinds, which she had enjoyed with Emily on the morning of her departure.

"I forbid you to marry him," Muriel announced. "In fact, I insist you rid us all of his presence at once!"

Augusta thought both Muriel and Sir Benjamin had overreacted that morning. Her hope was that in a few years, Muriel would outgrow her need for dramatic vignettes. But what of Sir Benjamin? If he did, indeed, have an unnatural affinity for citrus, how was Augusta to know if he loved her or her family's orangery?

"Oh no, Gusta, you must rid us of him." By the determined tone of Muriel's voice she was already formulating some sort of plan to be rid of him.

"It will have to wait. I am to meet Mr. Allendale for a boat ride on the pond." Augusta collected her parasol, gloves, and bonnet.

"He brought you to the Exeter Exchange, as I recall," Muriel mused. "I'm sure you won't need protection from any ferocious animals on our property."

"Unless he expects to find tigers hidden in the nearby shrubbery." Charlotte chuckled.

"I shouldn't think so, but you might beware of some kind of assault, Gusta," Muriel commented. "Not from the water but from your companion."

"A good afternoon to you, Lady Augusta, and to you, Mrs. Parker," Mr. Bertram Allendale greeted them at the edge of the knot garden ten minutes later.

"You and my niece may proceed, Mr. Allendale. I shall observe from here." Aunt Penny fastened the ribbons of her bonnet.

"Very well, Mrs. Parker." Mr. Allendale held out his

arm, offering to escort Augusta to the pond. "Good fortune is indeed shining down upon me. I am so very delighted to have this opportunity to spend some time with you, ostensibly alone. Your suitors have made themselves scarce and their number seems to dwindle by the hour."

"There are other pastimes at Faraday Hall besides keeping my company." Augusta tucked her parasol under her free arm. "You gentlemen seem to have no limits when it comes to entertaining yourselves."

"There may be other activities but none more important." A genuine smile filled with charm graced his face. "Ah, here we are. Is this our vessel?"

"It is. Do you approve?" Augusta had no idea what she would do if he did not, for there was no other boat available.

"It appears seaworthy." He strode onto the small dock and looked the boat over. "If you, and your aunt, will forgive me." Mr. Allendale arm-waved to Mrs. Parker, who stood in the distance, acknowledging her presence. He removed his jacket and deposited it, along with his hat, on the bench, and made quite the show of rolling up his shirtsleeves. "Although we are not chaperoned, I know that one is not far off, and I must prepare to take hold of the oars."

Augusta thought it might not take much encouragement from her to have him flex his muscles, to strike a pose or two for her amusement before he stepped into the rowboat.

After embarking, he reached out to help her step safely on board, and she sat at the stern, facing Mr. Allendale, who sat in the center. Augusta opened her parasol and rested it upon her shoulder.

Mr. Allendale used an oar to push the boat from the dock before taking his position. An almost audible grunt erupted from him as he began to row.

The boat pulled away, gliding with ease across the smooth surface of the water.

"This is lovely, is it not?" Hatless Mr. Allendale squinted into the sky and then glanced over his shoulder.

"It's a very nice afternoon," Augusta agreed. The boat pulled behind a willow tree, where sight of them might have been obscured for some short period.

Mr. Allendale stopped rowing and leaned from port to starboard.

"What are you doing?" An unsettling feeling, not of their circumstance but in question of his sanity, grew.

"I am merely testing the boat's stability." Mr. Allendale swayed to his left and right, doing his utmost to increase the motion.

"If you think you're frightening me, you are very much mistaken," Augusta cautioned him.

"Oh, come now, my lady, surely you must be a bit concerned. Perhaps you would like to sit closer to me?" He patted the space, the very small space, next to him. "Here?"

"I do not think that would be advisable." Especially for someone whose company she had growing doubts about sharing. She had thought him agreeable and admirable. She soon amended her opinion of him to odious and tyrannical.

He pulled in the oars and stood, rocking the boat from side to side with more animation.

"Mr. Allendale, what do you think you're doing?" The soundness of the craft did not worry Augusta. Her companion's questionable actions did.

"I just thought I'd stretch my legs." He then used the weight of his entire body. Water splashed around them, some into the boat as he leaned side to side.

Augusta cried out more at his audacity in attempting such a feat than in fear that their vessel should be over-turned. She dropped her parasol on her lap, clasped the sides of the boat with her hands, and increased the rocking motion. Mr. Allendale was not prepared for her attempt and lost his balance.

She watched his eyes fly wide open before he soared through the air, as if in slow motion, landing in the pond with a loud, crisp splash.

"What I really find worrisome," she shouted over the edge at him, "is that you are probably not as confident *in* the water as *on* the water."

"Lady Augusta!" Mr. Allendale's struggle soon ended and he appeared quite able to remain afloat. It seemed water immersion was not as dire as it was inconvenient. "Please, I beg you!"

Augusta stood, stepped about, and resettled in the center of the boat. She picked up the oars and paddled away. "I bid you farewell, Mr. Allendale, for I expect I shall not see you again. I'll make sure to have Huxley inform your valet that you'll need a dry change of clothes before he packs your trunks to leave."

Muriel came upon her aunt, who at one moment sat placidly, looking toward the pond, and the next moment sprang to her feet, quite agitated, and cried, "Oh, goodness!"

"What is it, Aunt?" Muriel ran to her side at once when her normally unflappable aunt panicked.

"Moo, dear Moo—quickly now! You must summon some footmen." Aunt Penny grasped her arm, urging her niece back toward the house but kept glancing over her shoulder. "Augusta and Mr. Allendale . . . they were rowing on the pond and there has been an accident. He has fallen in!"

"An *accident*?" The alarm Muriel once felt subsided. She gazed in the direction of the pond. Even without the aid of her opera glass she could see a single person in the rowboat, clearly Augusta, rowing toward the dock. "I'm sure he is fine, Auntie, he's hardly splashing at all."

"He has fallen overboard! Now, go—at once. You must send someone to rescue him."

"With Augusta there, I can see how he would need someone to save him." Muriel headed toward the house while Mrs. Parker moved in the direction of the pond. Once inside, Muriel alerted a pair of footmen to the emergency. They left immediately to aid Mr. Allendale.

Muriel strolled down the corridor toward the Grand Foyer. The house felt quiet with the majority of Augusta's suitors gone. The departure of Mr. Allendale would leave six.

The clink of china led her down the corridor and the murmur of many voices drew her toward the Oriental Parlor. Inside, Charlotte played hostess to Emily, Miss Randolph, Miss Olivia and Mr. Lawrence Skeffington,

Sir Samuel Pruitt, Lord Arthur Masters, Sir Benjamin Pelfry, and Lord William Felgate.

"Muriel," Charlotte called out. "Would you like to join us?"

"No, thank you, Charlotte." Muriel glanced at the lot of them and decided she was never more happy not to be included in their gathering. She backed from the doorway and continued toward the Grand Foyer, but not before she heard, from Sir Benjamin Pelfry, "Look there, they provided a dish of lemon slices for my tea!"

"Sounds splendid!" came Lord William Felgate's reply. "I'd like to try that!"

Muriel hurried away down the long corridor, hoping she could avoid overhearing any further citrus remarks. She came upon the two orange trees with their paltry offering of two oranges each. By tomorrow these trees would be stripped of their fruit completely.

"We'll stay in Bloxwich for a few days until I can arrange the marriage settlement with Miss Jessop's father, then we'll make plans for the wedding." Lord Marsdon, with his younger brother Sherwin by his side, descended the staircase. Both were dressed to travel.

Muriel thought it odd how a heavy feeling developed inside her upon seeing him, knowing that he was to leave Faraday Hall.

Mr. Lloyd noticed her once he reached the main floor. He leaned toward his brother and spoke before stepping toward her.

"Are you to leave, then?" Muriel could not very well deny she had overheard Lord Marsdon's announcement.

"I was hoping our stay would last longer. Indeed," Mr. Lloyd continued, "I had thought how very fortuitous it would have been if our siblings were to marry. We could have had many more discussions regarding the Romans and the Greeks, and compared their various works of literature."

"So your brother is to wed Miss Eleanor Jessop, is he?" Muriel could not imagine a more ill-suited young lady to become a viscountess and future countess. Muriel was saddened to see her new friend, if she could call Mr. Lloyd that, leave.

The only others she could engage in a worthwhile discussion were her brother, Fredrick, when school was not in session, and her father, who was far more busy recently than he had ever been.

"I am very happy to have made your acquaintance, Lady Muriel." A quaver in Mr. Lloyd's voice told her he was just as saddened by his early departure. "I do not know how long we'll stay in Bloxwich nor do I know if I shall return home to Lloyd Manor before the next term begins." He leaned close and whispered, "I shall be very happy to receive your missives once I return to school. I pray that Headmaster Keate takes your suggestion under serious consideration."

"Thank you, Mr. Lloyd." Muriel smiled. "I should, very much, like to continue our dialogue."

"If there is a matter of which I can be of service, please let me know." He flashed a shy, nervous smile. "Perhaps I will make the acquaintance of your brother."

"I shall write a letter of introduction," Muriel told him. He accepted her hand when she held it out to him and bowed.

"Sherwin," Lord Marsdon called out. "It's time to leave."

"Perhaps we will have the good fortune to meet again." It was clear young Mr. Lloyd felt self-conscious when a flush crept up his neck and washed over his face. He squinted a bit.

Muriel knew, without his glasses, he could not see close up clearly. He stared, quite focused on Muriel, as if committing her to memory. For they both knew it would be a very long time, if ever, that they should encounter one another.

Lord Marsdon handed Sherwin his hat, which he seated upon his head of dark hair, and with a last look and a nod, he and his brother left. Muriel did not follow them or look out the window to watch their transport pull away.

Moving down the corridor, her destination was the Music Room. She paused next to the orange trees, half-expecting their fruit to have disappeared while her back had been turned.

Muriel jumped when the door to her father's library pulled open, and she staggered back when she heard voices. Men's voices. Her father's and . . . who else's?

"I shall send word to Augusta, Lord Fieldstone, and you shall have your chance to speak to her alone. I wish you luck."

"Thank you, Your Grace."

Muriel dashed around the nearest doorway, hiding from Lord Fieldstone as he exited.

Where was Augusta? Outside . . . the pond . . . but surely not after "disposing" of Mr. Allendale. Muriel was quite sure she would find her sister in her bedchamber for some privacy to gain control of her temper.

But after what Muriel had just witnessed between their father and Viscount Fieldstone, it would be worth disturbing her sister.

Augusta would want to know.

Chapter Thirteen

Not two minutes after she had settled in her bedchamber, Augusta bade her youngest sister enter. Clearly,
Muriel wanted to know what had transpired on the pond
with Mr. Allendale. Not until Augusta set eyes upon her
sibling did she realize Muriel's agitation nearly matched
her own.

"What is it, Moo?"

Muriel was seemingly out of breath from rushing up
the stairs. Or perhaps her condition was due to the sig-
nificance of the news itself.

"Viscount Fieldstone has spoken to Father," she
blurted out.

They both knew what a private audience meant.

"How do you know this?" Augusta did not wish to rely
upon any type of hearsay, from servants or otherwise.

"I saw Lord Fieldstone emerge from father's library
with my own eyes just a few minutes ago." Muriel raised
her right hand as if to swear what she had witnessed was
the entire truth.

147

Augusta's knees felt as if they would not hold her up-right. She reached out for the edge of her dressing table and eased herself onto the chair.

The Viscount had received permission to pay his ad-dress to Augusta. But he couldn't possibly . . . Augusta was simply not ready to make a decision.

Lydia entered and handed a slip of paper to Augusta, which she read immediately.

Gusta,
   Lord Fieldstone wishes to speak to you. Please meet him in the Citrus Parlor at 3 P.M.

Papa

Augusta took a quick glance at the clock on her bed-side table—ten minutes. She swallowed, drew in a slow breath, and held the note out to her sister.

"So it's true!" Muriel gasped. "Gusta, what are you going to do?"

"What else can I do?" Augusta gazed once more into her mirror at her reflection. "I must ready myself to see Lord Fieldstone in the Citrus Parlor."

Some five or so minutes later—because she did not wish to arrive late—Augusta entered the Citrus Parlor. It was a room named for its numerous lemon, orange, lime, and grapefruit depictions. Trees and orchards of vari-ous colors—yellow, orange, and green—decorated the walls and the furniture upholstery and trailed across the ceiling.

Augusta sat, perching on the edge of the green-leaf patterned sofa, and arranged her skirt on the seat. Then she stood and paced to the window. Then she returned to the sofa, resetting her skirts, and tried to calm herself by counting the fruit on the wall.

She couldn't sit; she couldn't count. Augusta once again began to pace. She turned to walk back across the room toward the open door.

Lord Fieldstone was about to propose marriage. She was to be Viscount Fieldstone's . . . wife. Did the thought please her? Make her feel anxious? Terrified?

"Richard!" she cried out when she caught sight of him passing by the open door.

He halted and doubled back to her. "Gusta? What are you doing in there?"

"Please, don't leave," Augusta pleaded, nearly begging him. She probably would have if he had refused. "Stay with me. I'm waiting for . . . He's to arrive any moment now. I—"

"Who?" Richard stepped into the room, closer to her.

"Lord Fieldstone . . . he's already spoken with Father." What did she expect Richard to do? Hold her hand? Tell her she and the Viscount would make a perfect match? Did she even wish to hear those words from him?

Perhaps she wanted her good friend to promise that she would find as much contentment with her viscount as he had found with his fiancée, Miss Skeffington.

"He—" Richard stilled, and she'd never seen him look this serious. "Viscount Fieldstone, is it?"

Richard's presence had a calming effect on Augusta, and she was gratified he chose, of his own accord, to remain with her.

"I must wish you happy, then. If he is your choice, that is. He is a most fortunate man."

"Is he?" Her voice sounded weak even to her.

"Indeed he is." Although Richard's words were polite, Augusta could not believe he meant them.

"I'm not so sure." She confided in him—her long-time neighbor and childhood friend. "Could I marry someone who does not laugh?" Coaxing a smile from him on a daily basis would be a chore.

"From what I hear, you would need to tolerate his lack of humor."

Augusta stared at Richard, waiting for another comment, some wise words that might help her make the important decision regarding Lord Fieldstone's offer.

At that moment she did not see Richard as her friend and confidant. She studied his ruffled, light brown hair and his green eyes. He had always been there for her, when she was afraid or when she had gotten hurt. Augusta had never realized she relied on him so.

Only since she'd seen him in London had she realized just how handsome he was, how very—

What was happening to her? She had no idea why these strange thoughts were coming to her—especially now with an offer of marriage imminent.

"Take my hand," she whispered, sounding desperate. Augusta needed some stability. He reached out to her and she snapped, "No, don't touch me." She feared she might do something, say something rash in her confusion.

"I was just thinking back to when we were seven years old. Remember when we chased one another around the gardens, outrunning our siblings? Who would have ever believed . . ." He paused, looking thoughtful and sounding a bit sentimental. "Look at us now. Both adults, both betrothed." Richard nodded his head, acknowledging her unrealized position. "Well, you very nearly so."

"It is almost beyond comprehension." She turned and wrung her hands together.

"Sometimes I wish the situation were different. . . ." He gazed into her eyes; his smile faded. Augusta saw what she thought was *regret* cross his face, but only for a moment. "If our circumstances were— That is of little consequence." He cleared his throat. "What will you answer when Lord Fieldstone makes his offer?"

"I do not know." And she didn't. Augusta felt strangely numb. She would hear her reply when she answered the Viscount.

"Then I shall not be so hasty to congratulate him," Richard replied. "We shall see what becomes of Lord Fieldstone."

"Exactly," she agreed. "It would be most prudent to wait for the outcome."

Richard stepped closer and made to reach out with his hand to her again, only this time she did not cry out. "Gusta, I do wish—" His eyes and his voice softened.

"Lord Fieldstone!" Augusta announced upon his arrival.

Richard quieted, the momentum of his arm stopped, and he made a quick bow. "If you will both excuse me."

The Viscount entered and Richard left, closing the door behind him. Augusta was trapped in the room with Lord Fieldstone.

It was happening.

"Lady Augusta," he addressed her.

"Lord Fieldstone," she returned, acknowledging him.

Augusta had never noticed his overly stiff and formal bearing—everything about him seemed uncomfortable. "Won't you please be seated?"

These situations were always so awkward. Why did he not simply ask the question so she would know her answer? For at this moment, Augusta had no idea.

Lord Fieldstone sat at one end of the green-leafed sofa and Augusta sat at the other, leaving enough room for two more people to occupy the space between them.

"Lady Augusta," he began. "I spoke to your father, His Grace, earlier, and explained my position."

"Oh?" she commented quite dumbly. The room was growing warmer.

"You are the most charming lady of my acquaintance. You have wit, intelligence, and beauty beyond compare." He stared pointedly at her to assure her of his sincerity.

Stop. Please just stop talking. She did not wish to hear what he had to say.

"Even compared to the lovely Lady Charlotte I find you far more amiable, and you would exceed any expectation I could ever hope to find in my future viscountess."

Augusta's heart raced. Was this what *she* wanted? What she had dreamt of for herself? The panic she felt told her no.

She did not want the rank nor the flattery, which she did not think empty. Augusta was quite certain that Lord Fieldstone had meant every word.

Still, she did not think she could accept him.

He went on and on about duty and responsibility. Where were his sentiments of love? Had he no true affection for her as a woman?

And then she realized with complete relief that she harbored no warm feelings for him.

None at all.

She did not wish to marry him, and when he asked— *if* he ever got around to asking—the answer would be a resounding no.

"I must be honest as to my intentions," he continued. "As much as I have come to admire you."

Augusta remained silent and allowed him his say.

"I had hoped to find a bride and marry this year—you would be more than adequately qualified. Through no fault of our own, I believe, very strongly, that we simply do not suit."

What was that he said? Did he not *wish to marry her?*

"As I have mentioned before, you are all that is—"

"The combination of our personalities . . ." Augusta clarified, thankful that she would not need to turn him away. "I am quite at a loss to explain as to why . . . but I quite agree with you, my lord."

He looked as relieved as Augusta felt.

"I, too, find you all that is proper and agreeable." She glanced away to give herself a moment to gather her thoughts. "I must confess there is something that prevents me from forming a strong attachment."

"I thank you for your understanding." He inclined his head and stood. "Now I must bid you farewell and take my leave. I thanked your father for his hospitality earlier and now that we have discussed matters between ourselves, I can leave with a clear conscience."

Augusta stood to walk him out the door.

"It is unfortunate, indeed, that we did not make a

better impression on one another." She smiled at him. Something, it seemed, he was incapable of doing. "I believe we understand one another quite well."

"And if, by chance, you are to attend the Season next year, may I bespeak a dance at Almack's when we meet?" Viscount Fieldstone did not lack in charm, that much was for certain.

"You may, indeed, my lord." She could hardly refuse such a gracious gentleman the request. "I would be more than happy to make your acquaintance once again."

"Until the next time we meet, then." Lord Fieldstone bent low over her hand and then straightened. He displayed such a wide smile that it transformed his entire somber countenance.

Augusta found it so shocked her, it defied expression. She had no idea that leaving her would give him such joy.

Most of the guests had finished their tea and departed, leaving Charlotte in the company of Sir Samuel in the Oriental Parlor. Sir Samuel immediately stood when Mrs. Parker stepped into the room.

"Will you not sit?" he asked her.

"Is there any tea left?" Aunt Penny settled into a chair.

"Yes, of course." Charlotte poured a cup for her aunt, who appeared uncharacteristically distraught.

"Have you seen Muriel?" Aunt Penny took the cup and saucer, trying very hard to keep the porcelain set from rattling.

"We were denied Lady Muriel's company when she stopped by earlier." Sir Samuel glanced at Charlotte with what seemed to be a worried expression. Aunt Penny's nerves had not gone unnoticed by him either. "I'm sure she's much too busy with her studies . . . Hadrian's Wall, I believe."

"I had not realized you knew of my younger sister's interests." Charlotte regarded Sir Samuel with great fascination.

"Yes, we had quite the discussion about the Roman occupation in northern Britain," Sir Samuel replied. "From what I gather, she's more interested in people from the first century BC than those of us in the nineteenth century."

"She's still young." Aunt Penny's tone was one of understanding.

"Too young to care?" Sir Samuel wondered.

"At the moment, yes. I have every confidence that in a few years her interest will turn to young men, as most young ladies' do." Mrs. Parker sipped her tea and closed her eyes as if savoring its effects. "How were the guests this afternoon?"

"There seems to be a general pleasantness in the house." Charlotte tried to sum up her observations. "They keep well-occupied and have plenty to distract themselves, with or without Augusta's presence."

"All the ladies are appreciated by the gentlemen," Sir Samuel added. "However, you will notice that every gentleman who addresses Augusta has a distinct spark in his eyes whenever she is present. She clearly remains the favorite. Present company excluded."

"I wonder if any more of them have been excused since this morning." Charlotte had not had a chance to speak to Augusta or Muriel to learn of the present number.

"There was an unpleasant occurrence earlier." Mrs. Parker paused before saying, "Mr. Allendale fell into the pond."

"He's not with us anymore, is he?" Sir Samuel choked when he realized how dire his statement sounded. "I mean he'll be leaving Faraday Hall soon, I expect."

"Well before supper, I imagine." Mrs. Parker, looking most somber, rested her cup and saucer in her lap. "I would not wish to think ill of my own niece, but I cannot think the incident was an accident."

"Gusta is so naughty!" Charlotte could not help but scold her sister. "If only she would control her temper."

Sir Samuel coughed to disguise his sudden laughter.

"If she cannot"—Charlotte resigned herself to the possible outcome—"I doubt there'll be anyone left to keep us company for tea tomorrow."

Augusta collapsed onto the green-leafed sofa in the Citrus Parlor and leaned back, taking in a great breath of relief.

Thank goodness.

She felt immensely relieved by Lord Fieldstone's departure and grateful for his honesty. He was a man who knew his duty but would not be dictated to by anyone. He was quite a gentleman to admire, and she did admire him, but she had no wish to marry him.

Thank goodness.

"I say, is that you in there, Lady Augusta?" Sir Benjamin Pelfry entered the Citrus Parlor. Once he stepped inside, his attention shifted from her to the décor and he turned to take it all in with his eyes wide. "What a magnificent room!"

"Do you think so?" All at once the conversation she'd had with her sisters came back to her. It could not have been more apparent that Muriel had been correct about Sir Benjamin and his fascination for citrus. "It is rather magnificent, isn't it?"

There was a wild look of fascination on his face. Why, Augusta wholly believed that he had no notion she occupied the same room.

"Sir Benjamin?" she uttered, then tried again, a bit louder, "Sir Benjamin?"

"How robust these specimens appear! The illustrations are so very lifelike! The vibrant colors! And so perfectly circular!" He crossed the room to the wall and ran his fingertips across the images. "Oh, so real, one can almost see their tender, delicate leaves. They cannot withstand a frost, you know."

Sir Benjamin became quite oddly animated at the discovery of a roomful of illustrated citrus. How perfectly *deviant* he sounded. Muriel had not exaggerated his obsession.

Goodness. And Augusta had thought she might marry him?

Perhaps it would be best if Augusta were to give him some privacy while he continued to expound the virtues of the fruit.

Augusta closed the door behind her when she left and followed the corridor down to the Grand Foyer. She regarded the pitiful display of oranges on the trees flanking the arched window.

She plucked the remaining fruit and headed toward

the back of the house. Once outside, Richard came around the corner, from the parterre, and approached her just as she pulled the door closed. Once he spotted her, he removed his hat, tucked it under his arm, and called out to her.

Augusta welcomed him and observed that the two oranges balanced in the crook of her elbow and the one she held in her hand did not go beyond his notice. "Will you be so kind as to accompany me?"

He gave a shallow bow and did not question her regarding their destination. Augusta pulled the rind from the orange and allowed it to drop at their feet. Richard bent to retrieve it.

She stayed him with a hand to his arm and smiled. "Please, leave it." She motioned him down the path, to the left.

"If that is your wish." He could not have understood but did as she bid. "Pardon me for intruding into your personal matters, but might I inquire if you and Lord Fieldstone came to an agreement?"

Augusta could hear the interest in his voice. She had been smiling ear to ear, which might have given him the wrong impression, but the outcome did so please her. "Yes, we did." She allowed another piece of rind to fall from her fingers.

He glanced at her for permission to retrieve it. She gave none and he allowed it to remain. They stepped past the remnant.

"Am I to finally wish you happy, then?" He did not say this with a smile, as if he actually was happy for her. Poor Richard must have felt confused all the way around.

"Lord Fieldstone and I have come to the understanding that we do not suit. I believe he has left Faraday Hall." She scattered several pieces of rind during their stroll.

"Do not suit—you are *not* to marry?" Richard quieted, apparently shocked at the news. He exhaled as if relieved. "I thought for certain . . ."

Not only did it feel wonderful knowing she was not marrying the Viscount, Augusta thought it sounded splendid when Richard said the words out loud.

"Gusta, what *are* you doing?" It appeared that her companion had had quite enough. He stopped before they had reached their destination and reprimanded, "Your father will not approve of your littering the grounds. He does employ a substantial gardening crew but to intentionally—"

"It's a trap," she finally told him.

Richard stood not twenty feet from the knot garden that sat between the greenhouse and orangery. At the door of the orangery she dropped the final bit of rind and placed all three peeled oranges together to one side.

"A trap?" He stared at her and apparently could not think of what to say.

Augusta stepped back from the orangery doors to admire her display.

"As in *catching a husband*? That does not seem to make any sense at all."

"Not *catch* a husband, dear Richard. To *eliminate* one of the suitors."

It took him a moment but he appeared to understand

her intent. "And which of the unlucky gentlemen do you wish to rid yourself of?"

"Lord *Ce-treese*."

Richard furrowed his brows and, once again, looked quite puzzled.

Chapter Fourteen

Richard accompanied Augusta back to Faraday Hall, where she bade him stop in the Oriental Parlor while she penned a short note.

"Do you know how many of your suitors remain?" Richard asked. "And how many have fallen by the wayside?"

"Check with Moo," Augusta told him. "We both know she's keeping meticulous accounts on every one of them."

"I know she has a record of each suitor and the day of their demise. She has categorized their downfall in excruciating detail. I had thought you might also have a tally of your own."

Augusta straightened, holding the small sheet of paper to allow the ink on her note to dry, and replied, "No, I do not. I do not see the point when my sister keeps far superior records than I ever could."

Moments later Augusta led the way down the corridor to the Grand Foyer.

"What's happened to the fruit?" Richard commented upon seeing the bare trees. "I thought there were at least a dozen oranges here."

"There might have been at one time." Augusta was not about to confess her transgression. She had merely removed the *last*, not *all*, of the fruit.

Augusta, with Richard trailing behind, came across the butler, who seemed to have appeared merely because she was in need of him.

"Huxley, please make arrangements for Sir Benjamin to leave."

"Yes, my lady." The butler remained as if he anticipated further instructions.

"Then would you be so good as to have a footman take this"—she handed him a folded piece of paper—"and deliver it to Sir Benjamin? I believe he may be found in the orangery."

With a nod of understanding, Huxley left Augusta and Richard, who both turned upon hearing Mr. Lawrence Skeffington and Emily entering through the front door.

"Look who we ran into just as we arrived." Emily stepped to one side to reveal Lord Arthur. On his arm, Miss Olivia Skeffington was wearing a most fetching ivory-plumed bonnet.

Augusta was in the midst of finding fault with every one of her suitors. She recalled how Lord Arthur Masters was an aficionado of the arts. What could he possibly do to arouse her wrath?

"Perhaps we can exchange partners, eh, Wilbanks?" Lord Arthur chuckled in good humor and relinquished Miss Skeffington to the care of her fiancé. "What is your pleasure, Lady Augusta? A leisurely afternoon ride? A drive in a cozy curricle?"

"Perhaps a stroll outside, around the gardens," Augusta stated before he could make another suggestion. "Allow me to retrieve my hat and parasol."

Ten minutes later it was Augusta who dangled off Lord Arthur's arm. He led her through the knot garden and around the edge of the building until they came upon the large quatrefoil-shaped fountain located in front of the house in the center of the immense circular drive. Lord Arthur stopped to admire the view, almost as if he were contemplating a landscape that begged to be painted.

Water climbed a great height into the sky, over the heads of four cherubs frolicking in the large center bowl. From the corner pedestals four swans, with their wings outstretched, spouted water into the massive basin.

"This is quite delightful." The soothing sound of water obviously made an impression on Lord Arthur. "How very fortunate you are to live at such a beautiful place. I'm heir to Parkfield in Somerset, you know." He glanced at her. Had he hoped it impressed her?

"How nice for you," she replied rather curtly.

Augusta quickly scolded herself. She should not be taking out her annoyance for Sir Benjamin Pelfry, Lord Fieldstone, or Mr. Allendale on Lord Arthur. Lord Arthur had done nothing to deserve a set-down.

Her thoughts had been unkind. She decided she must treat him with greater care and with the respect he deserved. "Do you have such a fountain at Parkfield?"

"No, but I should like to build one. Do you mind if I were to take a closer look?"

"We are here to admire the views, are we not?" Augusta moved her parasol from her right shoulder to her left and motioned that they should proceed. She leaned against the side of the fountain while he examined one of the stone swans.

"Look at this detail. The striation of the feathers is so lifelike."

She had nearly forgotten how he had admired the various statues during their visit to the British Museum while in London. At least he could find enjoyment in something—unlike Lord Fieldstone.

"The curves of the neck and arc of the wings are simply exquisite."

And he only admired art instead of becoming obsessed with it, unlike Sir Benjamin Pelfry.

"How absolutely, how amazingly, lovely." Lord Arthur's voice had changed from an admiring tone to a silken croon. "Her skin is so very pale and as delicate as alabaster."

Thinking he had just about lost his mind, Augusta turned toward him. If she were not mistaken, his last remarks were not of the swans but of Charlotte, who strolled through the knot garden with Muriel.

Augusta felt her anger rise inside. She narrowed her eyes and pressed her lips tightly together, removing and collapsing her parasol. Lord Arthur was about to meet his end with the water, exactly as Mr. Allendale had, only with water much shallower.

Muriel caught some movement out of the corner of her eye. A sheet of water sprayed into the air and gracefully fell to Earth.

"Oh, look there!" Charlotte pointed across the way toward the front drive. "Someone must help him!"

"Send the footmen," Muriel, who had been through a water rescue recently, advised.

"Yes, yes, I will, at once." Charlotte ran back to the house to relay the message.

Muriel reached into her pocket and pulled out a small folded piece of paper and a pencil. By the time she had drawn a line through a name, striking Lord Arthur Masters, she spotted Charlotte trailing behind a pair of footmen toward the fountain.

"What's all the to-do about?" Richard came marching from the house. He stood with Muriel while Augusta strolled in their direction with her open parasol resting upon her shoulder. "Gusta, what has happened? How did Lord Arthur come to fall into the fountain?"

"He was completely oblivious to my presence and talking nonsense to the marble swan. Then I realized it wasn't the swan he spoke of at all. He was referring to Char-Char," Augusta scoffed. "I asked him if he preferred to spend his time with my sister rather than me. The only response he gave was to repeatedly coo her name, and I prodded him with the end of my parasol."

"You pushed him in?" Richard sounded shocked, but Muriel thought he shouldn't have been.

"He would not have lost his balance except he had leaned so far over the water to be even nearer to her." Augusta did not sound the least remorseful.

"That was most unkind even for you, Gusta," Richard scolded.

"Unkind? What do you call spouting adoring words, which I thought he had meant for me, while gazing across the green at Char-Char?" Not one word of blame was directed at Charlotte. "Men!"

Muriel glanced at the two remaining names before pocketing her small notepad and pencil.

"Lord Arthur was in your company and making calf eyes at Char-Char?" Richard sounded outraged. "That's inexcusable."

"Then I am not as irrational as you would make me out to be, am I?"

"I most sincerely apologize." Richard bowed his head respectfully. "However, it was very ill-done of you to have left him there to drown."

"Honestly, he could simply stand. The water rises only to one's knees."

"Char-Char did send the footmen to help Lord Arthur and, see there, she's looking after his welfare herself." Muriel pointed to the pair of footmen extricating the soaking Lord Arthur from the fountain with Charlotte looking on.

"I shall inform Huxley of Lord Arthur's impending departure. Then I must change my dress." Augusta indicated an area on her frock before heading inside. "I believe he may have splashed water on my skirts."

"So Lord Arthur is another one gone." Penny did not know the exact count of the gentlemen still residing at Faraday Hall, but there weren't many left.

"It was horrid, Aunt Penny." Charlotte followed her aunt to the *Librarium*. "Augusta pushed him in—on purpose."

"I'm sure she must have had a very good reason." Penny did not wish to condone the action but felt that her eldest niece was incapable of such impish behavior without due provocation.

"All I know is that Lord Arthur had not said one word against her." The tremble in Charlotte's voice betrayed how the incident had affected her.

Penny contemplated all that had transpired the last few days and the recent events within the short passage of time since their guests had arrived. "Faith, the house is so quiet. Have all the guests left?" She gazed out the window overlooking the parterre.

"Moo will know exactly how many suitors remain." Charlotte ran to the doorway. "There she is now—Moo!"

Muriel stepped inside and, as if by instinct, she knew the precise topic of discussion. "There are two left: Sir Samuel Pruitt and Lord William Felgate."

"Only two?" Charlotte sighed with disappointment at the sad news.

Penny could imagine either gentleman would make her niece a fine husband, but she had no idea what Augusta's feelings were regarding them.

Then there was the other side of the coin. Augusta did not have to choose. The Duke had made that quite clear. But no one wanted to be alone, especially an attractive young lady at Augusta's age. Especially since she'd seen, first, her cousin Miriam just wed and, soon, her friend and neighbor Richard Wilbanks following down the matrimonial path.

Below, in the garden, stood Richard. He held his hat and faced his fiancée, Miss Skeffington, who wore a bonnet with a tall ostrich feather. If Penny was not mistaken, there was some very serious discussion occurring.

"Moo, come here, will you?" Penny stepped aside, allowing Muriel an optimal view. "Will you please tell me what is going on down there?"

"Aunt Penny, *really.*" Muriel pulled the opera glasses from her skirts. "I thought you did not approve of my *eavesdropping.*"

"There is a time and place for it," Penny replied, "and this is exactly the right time. Miss Skeffington seems to be doing all the talking. What is she saying?"

Penny remained patient while Muriel brought Miss Skeffington into focus, and it took a bit longer for her niece to concentrate on the discussion itself.

"Miss Skeffington thinks their match may be a mistake," Muriel relayed.

Charlotte gasped. "Does she think our Richard is not good enough for her?"

"Miss Skeffington says that it took her some time to accept that she does not hold his affection."

"Richard does nothing but dote on her," Charlotte said, defending their friend.

"He assures her that he is completely devoted to her." Muriel backed away from the glasses and groaned. "He calls her *Livy.*"

"Keep watching!" Penny pressed, urging Muriel to continue. Under normal circumstances, Penny would declare this "activity" unacceptable, but she had a feeling they needed to oversee this private conversation and hoped Richard would, eventually, forgive them.

Muriel leaned forward, once again concentrating on the couple. "He is bound by duty, not affection, Livy says. Richard wants to know why she should think that, because he has great admiration for her."

"Richard would get on with anyone. He is the most amiable and understanding of men." Even Charlotte, who never took a dislike to anyone, sounded as if she were finding his fiancée tiresome. "I am beginning to think that Miss Skeffington does not deserve him."

"Livy wants to know if Richard would not wish for more for himself. She wants to know if he would release her from their engagement if she told him she had found love. Just as he had."

"She hands him the mitten and then blames *him* for falling in love with someone else? With whom?" Charlotte demanded. "Who does Richard love?"

"Do you not know? Can you not even guess?" Muriel replied for Miss Skeffington.

"Who is he in love with?" Penny and Charlotte said at the same time. "What is he saying?"

"Moo!" Charlotte pleaded, becoming impatient.

"Miss Skeffington believes that more exists between him and Augusta than a property line between our estates. She invites him to examine their longtime, close friendship."

"Richard and Gusta." Charlotte's musical laughter filled the *Librarium* with astonished delight.

"She thinks it's obvious and wants to know how he could not see it. When Gusta and Richard are together Livy sees the pleasure in his eyes. She accuses him of not gazing at her in the manner in which he observes Gusta."

"Oh, dear," Penny voiced, sounding quite guilty. She had noticed that several times since they'd traveled to London. As an older, and supposedly wiser, woman, she should have known better than to dismiss the awareness as a passing interest.

"And Livy says Gusta returns his attention." Muriel could not keep her opinion to herself any longer and burst forth with, "She knows nothing of Augusta. How could she make such an absurd comment? How could Gusta be in love with Richard? We would certainly have known if—"

"Muriel, *please*, we're missing their conversation." Penny cut her niece's commentary short.

An undignified groan emanated from Muriel and she continued. "Richard says he would never admit he has any feeling other than friendship for Gusta."

"You mean Richard really *does* love Gusta?" Charlotte giggled. "How lovely! This is wonderful!" She spun around with her arms out wide, nearly threatening to strike the bookcases.

"Richard never meant to hurt Livy," Muriel continued translating. "He agrees to calling off their engagement. Miss Skeffington is telling him—" She continued to watch in silence, her jaw slowly dropping open, until she gasped. "I don't believe it!"

"What? What is she saying?" Penny stepped closer to the window and watched the couple herself but could not discern their actions.

"Moo?" Charlotte nudged, insisting her sister tell them.

"Livy and *Lord William Felgate* wish to marry."

"What?" Penny and Charlotte cried in unison. Penny moved to the table and sank into a chair. How had that match happened right under their noses without their notice?

"She's stolen Gusta's beau," Charlotte sounded rather cross.

"Miss Skeffington says Lord William has made every effort to win her, and he's even drinking tea as to keep her company. Although he"—Muriel make a choking sound—"has learned to find it less offensive with a slice of lemon."

"Oh, no." Charlotte made a sigh of unpleasantness.

"Richard wishes her and Lord William every happiness."

"He would not be so cruel to deny them." Charlotte moved to the window, next to Muriel. "Poor Richard. What is he doing now?"

Muriel kept watch. "Livy says if he truly loves Gusta, he must find her and confess his affection."

"Yes, yes! He likes the idea," Charlotte concluded from his excitable behavior that must have been apparent for anyone to observe.

Penny returned to the window and rested her hands on Charlotte's shoulders as she stood behind her.

"Richard and Augusta . . . I never would have thought . . ." Charlotte bounced up and down with excitement.

Below, Richard stilled. His head and shoulders drooped.

"Moo?" Charlotte asked, but by her tone she wanted the answer just as much as Penny.

Muriel lowered her glasses when Richard walked away. "He thinks it might be too late."

Chapter Fifteen

Augusta spied the Wilbanks' carriage roll down the drive. It was only one of many journeys between Yewhill Grange and Faraday Hall over the last few days. The tall, ivory plume from Miss Skeffington's bonnet tickled the air and waved farewell. Richard had most probably accompanied her.

"Gusta!" Emily cried from the Grand Foyer. She stood before the tall, arched window and the fruitless orange trees.

Augusta moved down the corridor toward her friend.

"I've been looking for you. I wanted to tell you myself." Emily fairly glowed with excitement. "We're having a small celebration tonight. You know, just the family." She rose up onto her toes, as if she might float away from the felicitous news. "I'm to be married. Do say you'll come."

"Married! Em, that is wonderful." Augusta laughed and hugged her best friend. She softened her voice and asked, "Who . . . who is this most fortunate young man? And why have I not heard of this until now?" How could she have been so blind to her best friend's romantic entanglement? Had Augusta been so engrossed in her own drama she had not noticed?

Emily reached out and Mr. Lawrence Skeffington stepped forward.

"I could not be happier," Emily said and took hold of his hand with her own.

"I could not be luckier," Mr. Skeffington remarked, placing a kiss upon his intended's gloved hand.

"I am so very happy for you both," Augusta told them, and she sincerely, deeply was.

"We wish to wait until after Richard and Livy wed—they have their second banns read tomorrow and next week they can marry!"

So soon? It hadn't been sudden at all. Augusta had known it would only be a matter of weeks once they'd returned home. She tried to swallow but her mouth had gone dry.

"Then Mr. Skeffington and I shall follow them happily to the altar in another month," Emily explained. "You will come tonight to help us celebrate, won't you, Gusta? Say you will . . . you must."

"Of course I will." How Augusta would face *two* happy couples she did not know.

"If you will excuse us, we want to tell the rest of your family—the Duke first. We shall see you tonight!"

Augusta was so very happy for her dear friend. She moved down the hall toward the back of the house and out the door, and wondered if she would ever find equal happiness.

Muriel marched downstairs looking for Richard Wilbanks. She had something to say to him. If Charlotte or their aunt could not bring themselves to address him, to scold him, to point out the obvious course of action, she most certainly would.

"Lady Muriel." Sir Samuel Pruitt's polite bow and the motion of his arm indicated she should precede him down the corridor. "If you please . . ."

"How are you doing this lovely day?" As instructed when speaking to Augusta's suitors, revised after the *wagering incident* with Sir Nicholas Petersham, Muriel brought up only the weather.

"It is a remarkable fine day, and if the winds of fate chance to blow my way, I have hopes of it becoming one of the most outstanding days of my existence," he answered with particular glee.

"Really?" Muriel could not mask her wide-eyed reaction, since she doubted the weather had anything to do with improving his day, and she could not inquire further.

Keeping her tongue still was difficult but she maintained.

They stepped out the back door onto the terrace overlooking the rear gardens and stopped.

"I am in search of Lady Augusta," he commented. "You?"

"I am desirous of having a word with Mr. Wilbanks," she answered curtly.

"So now we part ways." Sir Samuel bowed again. "Good day to you."

An uneasiness wound its way through Muriel's stomach. Sir Samuel was "in search" of Augusta? And he had great hopes of today becoming one of the most "outstanding" days in his life?

Muriel did not like the sound of it at all. She needed to find Richard and do a bit more than nudge him into action. Surveying the gardens from this vantage point, she saw no trace of him. The *Lapidarium* would provide a superb view and she thought it was her best chance to see him if he should be about.

Before she arrived, Muriel heard him call out to her. "Richard!" she returned, seeing him come her way. He ran to meet her.

"It's Sir Samuel—" they said in unison and stopped at the shock of uttering identical phrases.

"He's going to ask—" they said together again, then at the same time, "for her hand—" and "to marry her—"

"What?" They squinted at one another in a juxtaposition of confusion and complete understanding.

"I saw Sir Samuel and your father shake hands. His Grace wished Sir Samuel luck in persuading Gusta to accept him."

"You must stop them." Muriel felt certain Sir Samuel would ruin everything.

"Stop them?" Richard regarded her and it seemed he had only just then realized her position on the matter. Muriel did not wish her sister to marry the baronet. "What transpires between Sir Samuel and Gusta is none of my affair. Perhaps she will agree to marry him. Perhaps he makes her happy."

What? Wasn't Richard the type of man to fight for Augusta? Muriel did not think there should be a duel, but a fierce shouting match and a few missed punches might be in order.

"I believe he is uncertain of her response. He said something about the 'winds of fate' . . ." She tried to recall his exact words. "I walked with him for a bit. We parted on the terrace. He headed toward the maze."

"The maze. Come on!" Richard grabbed Muriel by the hand and headed full speed to the *Lapidarium.*

"Rich-ard! Richard!" she cried out, trying to keep up with him. Not only was he taller, his legs were longer and—

She let out a high-pitched squeal in surprise when he lifted her from the ground. He tucked her under his arm, racing the rest of the way to the stone structure and up the steps before placing her on her feet once again.

He did not ask about her well-being or if she had enjoyed the journey but looked toward the house, then over by the terrace, presumably searching for any sign of Augusta and Sir Samuel.

"There they are, at the camel entrance." Richard stepped back and guided Muriel in front of him. "Get your glasses, go on."

Muriel reached into her skirt pocket, pulling out her opera glasses, pencil, and the folded paper with the list of names. "Hold this, will you?" She handed him the collection and pulled the glasses free, raising them to her eyes.

She caught sight of the maze and moved down its side, passing over the lion topiary entrance to the camel topiary where, at once, Muriel spotted Augusta and Sir Samuel standing at the opening.

"What are they saying?" Richard asked quickly, wasting no time, seeming as anxious as Muriel was to know what transpired.

Muriel turned to face him, lowering the glasses. "I cannot. I am forbidden to spy on my siblings. You know that, Richard."

"He's going to ask her to marry him. I must know her answer." He crushed the folded paper in his fist. The look of concern on Richard's face and the emotional crack in his voice was something Muriel had never heard. "Moo, she is everything to me."

Muriel completely understood what this meant to him, but shook her head, denying his request. "I cannot. Please do not ask me again."

If Richard was angry, he did not allow it to show. He simply held out his palm. "May *I* try, then?"

She laid the opera glasses in his hand and moved back, allowing him to achieve the best possible position, not that it would aid him in the least.

Sir Samuel Pruitt, only sixteen years of age, nearly three years younger than Augusta herself, was ready to do his duty. To carry on the family name. He currently held one of his grandfather's lesser titles of baronet. He was in line to take his father's title, Earl of Hampstead, and when his grandfather expired, he would become the Duke of Cubberleigh.

If Augusta understood correctly, he was most fortunate in finding a love match. But could Augusta claim the same?

"Lady Augusta," Sir Samuel pleaded, imploring her to give his troth proper consideration. As of yet she had not answered, but all the same, he seemed to know her doubts. "Tell me, is there truly no hope for me?"

"Sir Samuel . . ." Augusta did not know how to phrase her words. He had been devoted to her for so long, wishing and hoping that she might care for him above the others. To be honest, she did not. "You have been the most faithful, considerate, and amiable of the gentlemen. You deserve so much better than— You need a lady who adores you. I am not she."

"But I worship you!" he continued. "I could not hold a female of my acquaintance in higher esteem."

"But I am afraid I do not feel the same." Augusta saw the brightness in his eyes dim. "I am very sorry. You deserve so much more. You deserve to be happy, and I'm sure one day you will find a wonderful woman. She will feel respect and adoration for you as equally as you do for her."

His head fell forward and she could not see his expression. Oh, how she did not wish to cause him pain. But Augusta knew she could not accept his offer of marriage.

She smiled, trying her best to coax a smile from him. "Please believe me. I think this is the best for both of us." She nodded, renewed her effort to smile, and was rewarded with his brightening expression.

"Perhaps next year . . . if you should still wish to be married." Sir Samuel straightened with the restored hope. "I shall be seventeen by then."

"Your age does not concern me in the least. I simply believe we are not meant to be married to one another." She tried to bolster his confidence with, "You are very dear to me, and I should like to think of you as a great friend. I, or either of my sisters, can rely upon you, for both Charlotte and Muriel have only good accounts to recommend you."

"Please tell me, is there someone else?"

"No, there is no one." And that was the truth. "The house party has been an ill-conceived notion. I'm certain, as exceptional as the gentlemen are, I can honestly say there is not one who has laid claim to my heart."

"I see." The sadness in his voice returned. "But you are alone." His words sounded hollow, empty, just as she felt.

"I know," Augusta replied. She truly believed that being alone was far preferable to being with the wrong person, with someone you did not love.

After parting from Sir Samuel, Augusta wound her way into the maze and finally arrived in the center, feeling so very confused. She gazed up at the statue and wished, truly wished, her mother were here.

Aunt Penny had been all that was loving and did a wonderful job raising her sister's three daughters, but through no fault of her own, their aunt was not their mother.

Augusta sank onto the bench. At this moment, life was very difficult. As delightful, exciting, and trying as the house party had been, with fourteen eligible men in attendance, Augusta had not managed to meet a single man she wished to marry.

Emily and Lawrence Skeffington, how truly contented they looked. It was wonderful they had found one another. Augusta looked forward to celebrating their engagement. How lucky for Emily. She deserved to be happy in every way. As did her brother . . . the thought of sitting at the same table with Richard and Olivia Skeffington . . .

Augusta did not think she could face them—

She froze when it suddenly dawned on her. Augusta knew exactly . . . But it could not be. She stood, as if readying herself to run from the terrible truth that had revealed itself.

But it was impossible.

Richard?

How could Augusta have fallen in love with Richard Wilbanks? He was to marry Olivia Skeffington.

How utterly stupid she was. How could this have happened?

She had never wanted to fall in love with him. Richard had never attempted to engage her feelings. He probably thought no more of her than his own sister.

Augusta's breath caught in her throat as the rush of emotions threatened to overtake her. Tears of sorrow stung at her eyes.

What was she going to do? Augusta had to attend the dinner tonight with both of them present. How could she face him knowing what she knew now, feeling what she now knew was love for her dear, dear friend Richard?

Augusta swiped the tears from her eyes and drew in a steadying breath. She had to bury her feelings and wish him well, both him and Miss Skeffington.

"Gusta?"

Augusta spun around at the sound of Richard's voice.

"Are you all right?" Standing under the ivied arch, he stared at her.

Why was he here? His gaze felt uncomfortable and

intrusive. She did not want him near her, and above all, she did not want him to know she'd been crying.

"I was concerned about you," he said timidly.

"Concerned?" Had he known she'd just turned Sir Samuel down? Did he come to roast her about being unmarried, after all those gentlemen who had come from Town to court her? "Go ahead and laugh."

"Why should I laugh?"

"I've sent off most of the suitors and I'm destined to be alone." She felt contrary and especially did not want him feeling sorry for her. Augusta did not need his pity. "I shan't have anyone."

"I'm still here." He stared at her and she gazed back at him.

Something in his demeanor was decidedly different. Had she imagined it? Augusta felt unable to hang on to the resentment of her situation. She had so chided herself before he'd arrived.

"Thank you, Richard. I, too, value your friendship." It really did not matter if he married Miss Skeffington. Augusta knew he would always be her cherished friend. Nothing would change that. Not age, time, distance, nor marital status.

"I take it you've refused Sir Samuel."

"Yes, I did." Augusta raised her chin a bit higher and did not want to cry in front of him. Why did she think she always had to appear brave? "And I expect it will not be long before he takes his leave."

"I am glad they've all gone," he confessed. "I was certain from the start that you'd have none of them."

"Do not think you can—" Her reply died in her throat. "How could you—? *All* of them are gone?" Augusta blinked twice before regarding him with her eyes wide.

"I see that I have caught you by surprise for once." He smiled at her confusion. "Livy has handed me the mitten."

"Olivia Skeffington's cried off?" Augusta gasped. "What on Earth have *you* done to—"

"Now that's the Gusta I know, blaming me right off, before any of the facts are known."

"Well, she's done so for some reason, and if you haven't given her cause to rid herself of you, then what?"

"Lord William Felgate."

Augusta stared at him absolutely stunned and quite speechless.

"I don't mind really, ours was an arranged affair. She's all right. Livy, that is." He glanced down at the stone bench and continued. "We suited well enough, but now that she's fallen in love with Lord William, she's much better off. Surely you must see?"

Richard sounded so calm, not as if his heart had been shattered at all. Augusta thought, however, that it must have been. He had always been a very sensitive boy, who had grown into a sensitive man. Could he stand there and tell her that his broken engagement did not matter to him?

"Our fathers won't be completely disappointed, mind you. They wanted our families connected, and Emily and Lawrence seem to have worked the whole thing behind our backs. They're to be married."

"Yes, Em and Mr. Skeffington." Come to think of it, Augusta hadn't ever remembered them dancing together. How they had managed to find one another she did not know. "Em told me herself. But what of *Miss* Skeffington? How could she form an attachment with someone else while she was engaged to you?"

"Apparently she felt my affection had been in question. She felt completely justified in diverting her interest from me."

"You?" Augusta could not imagine. Honest, faithful Richard would not look at any other woman while betrothed to Miss Skeffington. If Miss Skeffington had noticed his roving eyes, why hadn't Augusta? "Who is she?"

She might have been able to accept his marriage arrangement. It had existed for years, and he was to be wed to someone he did not truly love. But to now hear of someone new that Richard had been attracted to, when all along she felt . . .

Augusta was almost afraid to hear the truth. She did not wish to hear that Richard could have true affection for some other female, other than his fiancée, other than herself.

"To be honest . . ." Richard cleared his throat, and the corner of his mouth lifted in a half-smile. "Livy did not like the way you and I laughed when we were together."

"That is very strange. We have known one another forever. I do not see how she could object."

"She did not like how comfortable we were when we spoke or the way we looked at one another." The closer he moved to Augusta, the softer his voice became. "Livy said we stared at one another as if there was *longing*."

"I certainly did not *long* for you," Augusta objected most wholeheartedly. At least she did not think she had previously, not before she realized she'd harbored an unexpected affection for him.

"Apparently you did, according to her." Richard stared at Augusta without blinking, without smiling. "I must confess, I did, secretly, long for you. I had no idea it was obvious."

Augusta's "oh" escaped on a sigh.

"So tell me, Gusta, can what Miss Skeffington said be true?" He stepped close and drew her near with one arm. "Is it possible that you could love me?"

Augusta stared into his eyes. If she said the wrong thing, it might drive Richard away. Above all, she did not wish to lose him.

It wasn't because she did not want to be alone or he might be her last chance to have a husband. Augusta did not wish to lose Richard because she truly loved him completely. She somehow must have always known, deep inside, they should be together.

"I do love you, Richard," Augusta confessed, fearing those might be the words that would cause him to flee. "I only realized it moments before you arrived. I feel so foolish. How could I not have known?"

"You could not be a bigger simpleton than I. I had no idea until Miss Skeffington so kindly informed me of the depth of my affection." Richard's smile grew across his face, beaming with the joy Augusta felt emerging from her soul. "What manner of dolt am I not to realize I have been in love for all these many months, nay, years perhaps?"

"Now what are we to do?" Augusta could do nothing else but smile at him.

"I will seek out your father and ask if I will be allowed to pay my addresses. I only hope he will not turn me away."

"I should not think so." Augusta thought of how much he had changed. He did not resemble the neighboring landowner's son, as he now looked the part of a proper suitor in his tailored jacket, breeches, and top boots. "I believe he will approve and place you at my mercy for the final decision."

"How can you be so sure?" Richard tugged at his vest and smoothed the crease in his sleeve as if nervous. "If my fate lies in your hands, I need not worry. You are as devoted to me as I am to you."

"You might be a bit overconfident of my affection. You have not even tried to kiss me yet." She played at seeming aloof and could not stop herself from teasing him. "How should I know that you truly care for me?"

"I've only just discovered I'd been in love with you. I had not even thought about kissing you yet," he remarked in near shock, but made to move toward her. Augusta hoped it was for the kiss she desperately desired.

"If you do not, you may lose me," she told him, hoping it would encourage him to act.

"I shan't want that to happen, not after everything we've just gone through." Richard hesitated. Perhaps he felt a bit nervous, unsure of how he should proceed.

"Take my hand." Augusta reached out for him, as she had so many times, but found something concealed in his fist. "What is this you have?"

Richard opened his hand, revealing crumpled paper. "Moo's list of your suitors." He unfolded and smoothed it as best he could.

Augusta glimpsed a column of names with a line through all but one. She felt not exactly guilty, but saddened that she had found that many gentlemen unsuitable.

"It was a silly idea, especially since I was right here all along." Richard proceeded to tear it in half and in half again, continuing until only tiny bits remained.

He drew Augusta nearer and whispered her name ever so softly. She gazed into his eyes and knew what was to come next. Eager to share their first intimate embrace, Augusta drew in a breath and waited. This was everything she had wished for: the familiarity, the warm affection, the closeness.

"We won't be needing this." With a single motion, he threw the handful of small pieces straight into the air.

Little white pieces, turning in the sunlight, looking very much like snow, hovered above their heads. Augusta giggled and Richard laughed.

Somehow it felt quite liberating, as if those gentlemen had been set free while she stood here with the only man she'd ever loved . . . Richard.

Richard pressed his lips to hers in a delicate, soft, loving manner, kissing her among the pieces of paper fluttering down around them. Augusta leaned into him, savoring their first kiss, and looked forward to the many they would share in the years to come when they would finally be man and wife.